SIREN SONG

A STANDALONE NOVEL OF MERMAIDS, CURSES, LOVE, AND STRONG WOMEN

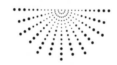

AUDREY FAYE

COPYRIGHT

DEDICATION

To the two years
that changed my life...

and to the people
who were in them.

CHAPTER ONE

*T*hree more pages and she was a free woman.

Or at least as close as a lowly post-doc ever got to freedom.

Holly took the last few steps toward the tiny office she shared with Jade Gleason, ready to get her Friday-afternoon self in gear and finish the paper she was working on so her weekend could be sixty hours of continuous sloth and gluttony. Or full-costume rehearsals and gobbled fries, but that would be fun too.

Just one of the many sacrifices she made for her art.

"Enter at your own risk."

Holly paused at the door and grinned at her best friend. Post-docs weren't always that friendly with each other—too much competition for the very few jobs that paid a living wage and didn't require any vital organs or firstborn children to close the deal. Jade was different, though. Her family had more money than an island of deities, and she wouldn't be working in the hallowed halls of academia much longer.

In ten years or so, Holly fully expected to see the woman currently making a paper-airplane catapult out of drinking straws to be running half the known world. "Your family's branching out into weapons of mass destruction?"

Jade carefully adjusted something on one of the straws. "Not as far as I know."

Uh, oh. Holly knew that tone. "Your father called." It wasn't a question—only one person could put those lines between her best friend's deep-brown eyes.

"Yeah." Jade pushed down on the business end of her catapult and loaded a paper airplane. "Look out, the aim on this thing isn't fine-tuned yet."

Story of the Middle Ages. Holly ducked reflexively and then winced as the sacrificial flier crashed into a wall and drifted to the floor, nose bent seriously out of shape. "I think you need an engineering consult." Or a father who quit trying to drag Jade off to do her duty to clan and country, but a cute engineering post-doc would be a lot easier to come by. Or maybe one of the ancient history geeks who knew how the Greeks and Romans built things, anyhow—Haversham's researchers didn't tend to run to folks who knew how to do anything modern.

Then again, catapults were pretty old-fashioned.

Holly swung her computer bag up onto the battered antique she called a desk and pulled out her laptop. Three pages. Freedom.

Jade retrieved her mashed paper airplane and dug two cans out of the tiny fridge that served as beverage cooler and occasional petri dish overflow, the latter being the reason that Holly didn't consume anything from the fridge that hadn't emerged from a vacuum-sealed can. She caught the fancy

Italian soda Jade tossed her way. "Are we out of root beer?" Her tastes tended to run to more plebeian forms of sugar.

"Pretty sure Tomas has been raiding your supplies again."

Tomas was the hot linguistics guy down the hall, but sexy abs only excused so much beverage theft. "I'll talk to him."

Jade grinned. "You can take my catapult if you want."

Not until it had an actual aiming mechanism. Which, given that her office mate's area of study was Middle Age biologicals, and not of the weaponized kind, might take a while. "Can you rig it so that it shoots anyone who opens the fridge door?"

"Oh, sure."

Holly laughed at her friend's eye roll. The fridge was closer to Jade's desk, so she'd be the one running the catapult gauntlet. "Not sure that's gonna scare a thief who's willing to brave your petri dishes anyhow. Hasn't your new lab fridge arrived yet?" Jade had very well-equipped lab facilities down the hall—or at least, they were well equipped for the work she was supposed to be doing. No one had ever accused Jade Gleason of keeping her research too narrow.

Which was all fine and good until she brought some of her pets home with her. Haversham's health benefits were really good, but they probably didn't cover bubonic plague.

"I put in a grant application." Jade's voice was getting drifty, the way it did when she was thinking about three things at once.

Holly followed her friend's gaze over to the trio of African masks gracing the top of a filing cabinet that had probably lived through the Middle Ages. Their sharp cheekbones and slashing beauty could have easily made them some of Jade's ancestors. "What?"

"Nothing." Jade shrugged and turned back to the stack of archeology journals on her desk.

Holly rolled her eyes. "Never lie to a storyteller."

That got her an amused snort. "You study stories—that's different."

Not as different as she tried to make people believe. "I'm an actress, too, and I'm totally on to you. Out with whatever it is." If it had to do with the very annoying father figure in her best friend's life, Holly was going to take the sharpest and pointiest of the African masks and go on a rampage. "Your dad being a jerk again?"

"No, actually. He invited me to dinner on Sunday."

That was far scarier than Daddy Warbucks being a jerk. "Don't go."

Jade tilted her head slightly toward the African masks and looked a little sad. "Not all of us can just decide to put our parents on ignore, sweetie."

It was the gentle tone of the words that caught Holly. She leaned over to get a better view of whatever had caused them —and saw the pendant. Hanging where she'd last left it, over the dude on the end with really big ears.

Just the latest resting spot after her most recent, very short-lived attempt to wear it. The pendant had been a final gift from her mother's estate, sent on her twenty-first birth-day, almost two years after a stretch of road in the middle of nowhere had claimed the only parent Holly had ever known.

Almost a decade later, it was a symbol of daughterly avoidance.

"Still not wearing it, huh?"

This was so not the direction Friday afternoon was supposed to go. There was a reason they generally banned conversation about parental units in this room. "I have three pages to write to finish this paper. I need to get on them."

"Holly." One word, even gentler than before. And the steady, non-judgmental offer of understanding that had been one of the reasons they'd become friends in the first place.

"I can't." Holly looked up and tried to keep the whine out of her voice. "It creeps me out, okay?" It had since the first day it had arrived in a fancy jewelry box that some lawyer's secretary decided was the appropriate vehicle to deliver a gift from the dead.

The lines between Jade's eyes creased again. "Because it was hers?"

No, although that would be a convenient excuse. This office was no stranger to parental baggage. Holly stared down at a corner of her desk and sighed. "You're an archeologist, not a therapist, okay? Yes, I know the pendant is my mother's. Yes, I know it was her dying request that I take it and wear it always. Yes, I know I'm a really shitty daughter for not doing that."

It wasn't the grief or the memories or the strained relationship she'd always had with her mom that were the main problem, however. The thing gave her the heebie-jeebies when she wore it. Literally.

A paper airplane nearly clipped her nose. "I didn't say any of that, and you know it."

Holly looked over into the sympathetic green eyes that would one day run Gleason Worldwide and squirmed. "I know. Can we drop this, please? I have to finish this damn paper, and then full-costume dress rehearsal starts tonight."

Jade grinned. "Want me to drop by with a crate of French fries?"

It had always been like that, ever since the third month of freshman year, when her elegant, sophisticated roommate had walked in on the sobbing puddle of a nineteen-year-old who had just learned she was an orphan. Ever since then, Holly would sometimes try to get prickly and cranky and Jade would disarm her with food, fancy soda, and the fact that she really cared.

Holly was well aware that the goodness of her current life had a lot to do with the sheer persistence of one Jade Gleason. "If you show up, Monster will trip over every cable we have, Kirk will walk into a wall, and Amanda will forget every third line of her solo." The hazards of a friend who could have graced the modeling runways with her chocolate skin and wild beauty. Glitzy packaging for a ridiculously kind heart.

Jade's eyes twinkled. "Kirk's pretty cute. So's Amanda."

If anyone on the Inkspot theater crew ever managed to nab her best friend, Holly's bet wouldn't be on either of those two. Monster, with his dogged efficiency, quirky sense of humor, and steady supply of Jade's favorite yogurt-dipped pretzels had a far better chance. Which still left the odds at miniscule. Anyone Jade liked automatically ended up in the crosshairs of Gleason Worldwide, and as far as Holly knew, her best friend had only ever put one person there. He'd run screaming within the week.

Just one more reason this office wasn't very fond of Daddy Warbucks.

"How's your princess coming along?"

Holly tucked her woolgathering back into captivity. Mostly she tried to keep it on a tight leash—the hallowed halls of academia weren't all that kind to dreamers. That's what the stage was for, and she'd be getting a serious fix of that over the weekend. "This one's pretty simple." When you'd played one flaky, fluttering damsel in distress, you'd pretty much played them all.

Jade raised an eyebrow. "Who's picking the next script? You need a challenge."

Probably, but finding the energy to make that happen wasn't all that easy. And the flaky princess had some nicely lyrical solos and one really fun moment of hysteria that had been doing a nice job of taking the edge off a volcano that Holly intended to keep on ignoring. "I need to write more words on the antecedents of feminism in Viking mythology. The theater stuff is just icing."

The acting wasn't icing, and they both knew it—but on a Friday afternoon where they could both smell the end of a very long week, Jade wasn't likely to argue.

Holly reached for the bottle of ibuprofen on the corner of her desk and took three. Her legs had been aching all day long, and that needed to stop.

Freedom beckoned—and French fries.

CHAPTER TWO

*H*olly walked into the black, dusty interior of the Inkspot theater, leaned against a pockmarked wall in the back, and felt herself exhale.

Or rather, felt herself sliding into her other skin. Her alter ego came most fully to life here in this cavernous, beat-up space that housed the best community theater group in five hundred miles. Or so they hoped, anyhow. Ticket sales were always strong, and the locals had lots of other choices. New England didn't suffer from lack of budding artists—and aging ones—willing to spend countless hours practicing to entertain their fellow human beings.

This particular motley collection had accepted her eleven years ago when she'd been a bright-eyed freshman with a few high-school musicals under her belt and the vague idea that she might want to make a living on the stage one day.

That wasn't ever going to happen—Holly knew better now, and she liked eating and paying her rent too much to deal with the starvation-level earnings of most serious actors.

She loved the camaraderie of a group of people who lived for their time on the stage and had made peace with not making any money doing it. Here, theater was purely about telling stories, about embodying them and making them come to life for the pure, sheer pleasure of it.

She smiled—in the pretty decent life she'd assembled for herself in the last decade, this part was one of the unchallenged crown jewels.

"Hey, lazypants—you going to stand there holding up the wall all night?"

Monster nearly rolled his trolley, laden with scenery backdrops and half the township's antique weaponry, right over her toes. Holly moved with dispatch—she knew how unwieldy the trolleys were to drive, and Monster tended to favor speed over minimizing wall dents.

Not that these walls would care. It was entirely possible that the Inkspot had once done duty as a nuclear bunker. Two-foot-thick concrete walls and nary a window in sight. However, it had decent acoustics, held lots of people, and had been theirs to use in perpetuity for longer than she'd been alive, thanks to some rich little old ladies who had enjoyed their evenings out at the theater and their chance to turn an eyesore into an act of public generosity.

Holly wasn't sure the cheerful murals on the outside did a lot to disguise the bunker, but it had turned the Inkspot into a landmark of sorts. One with a story, and she'd always been a sucker for anyone or anything with a tale to tell.

Monster elbowed her in comradely fashion as he rolled past her toes more gently than usual. "Still daydreaming, Sparky?"

She grinned—the man who bossed their backstage around

didn't talk much, but he had a new nickname for her every night. "I kind of liked Ophelia." It had amused her to no end to hear that one coming out of the mouth of their stocky, grounded props master.

"Ophelia's some wishy-washy dame who eats soft-boiled eggs for breakfast and lets her teacup poodle pee on other people's flowers."

She managed not to dissolve into giggles—mostly. "Dibs on Ophelia when you write that script." With lines like that, he should be writing.

He snorted at her over his shoulder. "Matt says we roll with your sniveling-princess-in-the-tower scene in ten and to see if you can find Romeo by then."

Holly grinned as someone new to the Inkspot's flock barely missed losing a limb to Monster's trolley, quickly followed by Gillian stepping in to save the pale teenager. Gillian was a theater lifer who changed personas as often as she changed her underwear. She would have fun playing mother hen for a while.

Holly had more important things to do, like finding her co-lead and figuring out how far she could lean over the newly constructed balcony without landing in the fake flowers or impaling herself on Ian's sword. The man was a great actor and a decent singer, but he was a menace with a weapon in his hand. Rumor had it that his wife had banned even tinfoil swords in their home. Something to do with their youngest son and narrowly averted blindness.

Which meant Ian only got to bust loose when there was a role requiring a swashbuckling love interest, and that had a whole lot to do with why he closeted himself with Matteo each winter to pick their scripts for the following season.

Holly just wished she didn't have to play quite so many princesses in distress so that the man could have his fun.

"Hols!" Matteo, the gangly guy with hair straight off Einstein's head, and also their erstwhile director, waved wildly at her from stage left. "It's about time you got here."

She was at least fifteen minutes early. "Papers to write, bosses to keep happy. What's up?"

"You warmed up?"

No, but her voice never required a whole lot of that. Like most community theater types, she sang a little, danced a little, and happily produced any of them on command in order to get her time under the spotlights. Holly picked her way through the floor flotsam and rested her elbows on the edge of the stage. "I cursed at a couple of drivers on the way over—I'm ready to sing."

"Good enough." Matteo crouched down in front of her and pitched his voice a lot lower than it had been. "Do me a favor and stand in the corner and practice your duet with me, would you? Ian's still flat as hell on the middle part, and I'm hoping that if he has a listen to it done right, we won't be here until midnight."

Pitch corrections rarely sank in by osmosis, but Holly knew better than to argue with the director on the first night of full-costume rehearsals. If he wanted her to sing something she already had note-perfect, she'd sing. It wouldn't be a hardship—Matteo had a pretty decent voice, and he'd never once stabbed her accidentally with his sword. "Sure." She swung a leg up and levered herself onto the stage. Her legs protested, and she made a mental note to take more ibuprofen as soon as she got the chance. It was likely to be a long night.

Matteo headed for the back corner and pulled up an app

on his phone to give them their starting note. Not something Holly needed—one of the weird skills she'd been born with was perfect pitch. She followed him into one of the Inkspot's darker recesses, already hearing the soft B-flat inside her head, and hummed quietly when the phone agreed.

"From the top?" Matteo looked at Holly like she might argue with him.

She refrained from rolling her eyes—her supervisor at work might occasionally find her intractable, but she was a stage director's dream. Punctual, malleable, and the last time she'd forgotten a line she'd been three feet tall and high on Valentine's Day candy.

All that mattered was that she got to live the stories. Tell them, channel them, be a part of their living, breathing fabric. Even the three-foot-tall version of Holly had lived for those moments. She could already feel it rising, the magic from deep in her belly that only turned on when she was about to step out of her life and into something bigger.

Matteo smiled as her slow opening notes whispered out into the theater. The first lines didn't call for volume. Holly's character was a spoiled teenager in the throes of her first love, denied the bliss of looking on her beloved. The song eventually worked its way into a full-blown royal temper tantrum, but it started sweet and light. The teasing, delicate flutters of a girlish heart and its swooning beats of love.

Which sounded foolish until you were inside it—and Holly's one great talent on the stage had always been her ability to climb inside a part and wear it for her own. She'd never had anything more than a passable voice, but she knew how to use it to make an audience believe. This song was no exception. She'd never been one of those teenagers who swooned after boys or girls or anything in between. But in this moment, she knew exactly what it felt like to be that girl, and her job was to make sure that everyone who could hear her knew it too.

She built the volume a bit, swelling into the first shiftings of those girlish flutters into something stronger, deeper, more passionate. The heady rush of it—and the fear. And then backed off as she reached the end of the opening verse. Matteo would join her for the next part, and his voice was true, but he lacked her experience in producing enough volume to hit the slightly deaf ears in the back row. Good harmony was only as strong as the quietest singer, and the whole point of this exercise was to educate Ian. Holly ignored the fact that her co-lead was probably swinging a sword around backstage, endangering the curtains and utterly ignoring their little demonstration. Lots of people would be giving their director headaches tonight, and she didn't need to be one of them.

She smiled as Matteo hit a particularly sweet phrasing. He might not have the face of a lovesick swain, but he understood the story they were trying to tell. She let her notes float to mix with his. It was going to be a good night—exactly the kind she needed after a week of paper writing and intellectual jousting.

Freedom, Holly Castas style.

CHAPTER THREE

*D*edra leaned over the edge of a low rock and reached down into the cool waters, picking up a handful of wet, white sand and letting it run through her fingers. *The voice wasn't bad, but the girl didn't have a clue what true passion was yet.*

She listened, tail swishing, to the dying notes of a pretty song sung by a foolish girl, and tried not to remember just how many times she'd done this.

How many times she'd failed.

The old siren shifted, seeking comfort from the dark gray rocks of her favorite cove, or the favorite one she had left, anyhow. Too many of them were infested these days with small white sailboats and passengers too willfully dense to believe anything their eyes might see. She'd learned long ago to stay out of their way.

Once, her kind had been revered. Feared, even, by those too foolish to hear beyond the tales told in bars by deckhands too drunk to remember which side of their pants they'd pissed on last.

These days, she was all too likely to be ignored.

If only curses could die so easily.

She trailed her fingers in the waters again, thoughts drifting in the patterns laid down by the ebb and flow of the tides and the grinding sands of time. The familiar drag of despondence settled over her like the cloak she'd once worn in human form, one fitted to her shoulders all too well. There was a tiredness as she faced the work about to come, one that didn't used to be there.

One she was deeply afraid she couldn't fight much longer. A thousand years might not show on her face, but she could feel them in her bones.

Her power was feeling the years too. It was getting harder to hear those of her blood, to reach out to those of her line who needed to step up to the call of a four-thousand-year-old curse and take up the warrior's burden so others would be spared.

To step up so that she might finally step down.

She waited for such a one.

She would not do like all the others had done. She would not give up, even if those of her blood had moved away from warm sands and ocean tides and anything else a reasonable mortal should want. Why on earth people had ever moved inland, she would never understand. They would never feel the waves moving in time with their blood, never feel the waters dancing at their fingertips. It was madness that caused people to live in a place where the air froze their cheeks and the water existed only as salt-deprived, captive lakes and contagion-filled rivers.

The kind of place where mothers named their progeny after bushes with silly red fruits. Dedra sniffed. In her day, children had been given names full of auspice and meaning. In this day, meaning was lost in a deluge of information that didn't matter, the inexorable march of centuries where belief had fought a war against the shallow, inflexible waters of rationality and lost.

And her sisters had paid the price.

All of them.

She sensed a single, salty tear rolling down her left cheek, and felt a vague moment of surprise that she had any left. A thousand years was a long time to cry.

Dedra. She'd picked her name because it meant sorrow.

She hadn't known then that the sorrow would never end.

CHAPTER FOUR

*M*irena could feel it—the call of the moon, the tug of the sea. It was almost time. Carefully, she checked the small packet tucked in at her waist, the one that held the meager amount of food she'd been able to filch from the kitchens. On the eve of a full moon, hunger was far better than a beating. Her legs still ached from the last one.

Tonight, nothing would ache anymore.

Assuming she could actually make it past the village guards. Getting out hadn't been a problem, but sneaking back in might be. The bandits and brigands had been getting bold lately, and the Sinchin had ordered extra patrols. Which she only knew because Cook had been in a dither, ordered to produce extra guard rations with not enough warning even to get a good soup going, and all the house staff had moved around at a whisper.

Cook in a dither was only marginally better than Cook in a violent rage—and one could become the other with less warning than the time it took a candle to flicker.

She shivered as she walked the dark path, her bare feet feeling their way through the strange shadows cast by the moonlight. Cook was not nearly the worst of persons, and Mirena wasn't going to think about that any more tonight. These were the few hours each month she got to escape from the kitchen and all that came with it, and bringing it along in her head wasn't going to help anything. Or that's what Mikel would say, anyhow. He was as solid as the earth he planted in, and he never worried about anything that wasn't right in front of him.

Just one of the many reasons why she loved him and yearned for the day when they would be handfasted. One more harvest, or maybe two, and then Mikel would have worked off the lease-price on a small plot of land of his own. *Their* own.

And then she could have a life worth living again.

Until then, this would have to do.

She paused at the top of the goat path that would lead her to the hidden cove. The sea crashed against boulders lying unseen beneath her in the dark. Mirena imagined she could hear words in their discordant sounds. A hissing argument, maybe, or weeping.

Mama would roll over in her grave if she could see where her daughter wandered.

Mirena started forward slowly, her feet finding the trail in the dark that she knew was there. It wasn't much easier to see the footholds in daylight, and it was far easier to see the sharp rocks below that would catch her if she slipped. Here, under the moonlight, she could focus only on the soft glow and the pain in her legs.

Normally, she tried to ignore the aching, but somehow, knowing that relief was coming very soon, the pain seemed to turn itself into sharp knives, stabbing her with every small movement.

It was a family thing—Mama's legs had hurt too. Always that feeling of having been trampled by horses, some days worse than others. If they had to have a family curse, at least they could have been dealt a more interesting one. Like her friend Grisha. All the green-eyed babies in her family had the sight.

Maybe the sight would have kept Mama safe.

Mirena bit her lip as her toes slid on a foothold, remembering the soft brown hair and sad eyes of the woman who had raised her, loved her, and one day had simply not come home. Maybe her legs had finally given up, laid themselves down at the side of a path in the hills one day and refused to go on any longer.

It had been two days after Mirena's thirteenth birthday, the one when she had gotten a job at the big house. The one that meant a child alone in the world might survive long enough that she could someday marry Mikel and have his babies. Working at the big house was warmth and safety and enough food to eat, even in the coldest months. Even Cook in a rage was better than a belly that had seen nothing but weak gruel for a month.

Sorrow rose in Mirena's heart as she caught her first glimpse of the cove's quiet waters. Ships wrecked often on the rocks beyond, but here, there was an odd and wild kind of peace.

She'd come here the first time a week after Mama had

disappeared, pulled by a bright moon and an awful loneliness and a song that nobody else's ears could hear. She had imagined she was sinking into madness, and she hadn't cared. For five years now, she'd made the journey, and if it was madness she faced, it did not pull her in any deeper. Only this far, that she might come sit by the water's edge under the light of the full moon.

Mikel would be angry if he knew she'd come again. He wanted her safe, and wandering the hills in the dark, especially on a night when the moon was full and bright and brigands grew bold, was pure foolishness.

Mirena gripped a stubby root she knew to be firm and solid and lowered herself over a jutting edge. Her Mikel was a very good man, but he didn't understand the pulls and aches of a woman's heart. He knew the quiet pleasure of the first plants creeping up through soil he'd tilled in spring, and the satisfying ache of muscles that had worked hard all day to put away food for the dark months. And his eyes filled with something akin to joy when they looked at her and saw the love she felt for him.

She would sit by his fire on her next evening off and let him rub her legs. It was something that would make the village ladies chatter, but with Mama dead and gone, there wasn't really anyone to care. The chatterers were simply jealous, or yoked to a man too dim to offer a foot rub and gentle conversation.

She'd fallen for Mikel's voice first. He'd never been the most handsome boy in the village, or the one with the brightest eyes. He'd always been a hard worker, but her silly young heart wouldn't have beaten faster just for that. No, it had been his voice, full of the warmth of a meadow on a long summer's day. It had promised her that under those broad shoulders and stalwart face beat a heart that understood softness. And so she had kissed him one day on a goat path in the hills, and when he'd kissed her back, she had felt someplace inside her ribs open and be glad.

Mirena shook her head as she took her first steps, legs shaking badly from the descent, onto the sand that glowed near to white, even in the dark. Always, she thought of Mikel here. Something about this place sent her heart to foolish fancies. She reached for the packet at her waist. It was probably just the hunger—she hadn't eaten since morning, and that had only been a crust of bread and the rind of a cheese so aged, she could still taste it.

That part wasn't Cook's fault. She had laid out a decent morning's rations for her kitchen workers, but Mirena had passed hers to one of the young boys running a message to the village. Tirenne was sick, and the soft bread from the big house soothed the old healer's belly better than the rougher grind everyone else lived on.

It wasn't kindness, or not only that. Mikel's youngest brother had caught the rattles in the winter, and Tirenne's plasters had kept the child alive. That was an obligation that would take a long while to pay in full, and Mirena was determined to do her part.

Just as she was apparently determined to risk beatings and brigands and the sad, disappointed eyes of the man who loved her. She reached for the respite of a large, flat rock near the water's edge, her legs nearly done. This wasn't worth it—and yet, she couldn't stay away.

She tilted her head up to the full moon, letting its cool

light kiss her face, and then she turned her gaze out over the waters and waited. The song would come—it always did.

At first, all she heard were the watery melodies of the gently lapping waves in the cove and the fierce, crashing ones beyond. She stretched out her legs on the rock's hard surface, grimacing as she moved. The climb down had been wet tonight, and particularly treacherous. She imagined Mikel's firm hands kneading the pain away, much as she kneaded bread dough in the dark each morning.

In her imagining, she let his fingers roam farther than the handspan above her ankle that she'd deemed permissible until they were handfasted.

The song from the waters rang with a slightly crazed note of laughter.

Mirena's eyes snapped open—it wouldn't do to fall asleep on the rocks. Returning late would earn her a beating if she was caught. Not returning at all would lose her the place in the kitchens that meant the difference between warmth and reasonably functional legs and the life of a hungry cripple in the village. Mama had always kept a warm fire, and one day Mikel would because he loved her, but no one else had precious wood to spare.

Not that her legs hurt right now. Mirena smiled and breathed in the wondrous feeling of limbs that stretched freely toward the water and did not hurt. It was only in these moments that she understood how deeply their aching permeated the rest of her life.

The song coming over the water was particularly eerie tonight. It sent shivers up her backbone, the strange, almost discordant harmonies that made her want to dance and scream and weep all at the same time.

She didn't know if it was one voice that sang, or a whole village, but it spoke of unfathomable longing and a torment she couldn't possibly understand—and yet did. They sang of hearts that ached as deeply as her legs. And their pain somehow chased hers away for a while.

CHAPTER FIVE

*H*olly woke up hard, fast, and out of sorts. The dream that held her in its grip was fleeing, leaving behind only fragments. A young girl on the rocks, listening to eerie, unearthly music that even now sent shivers racing up Holly's spine, despite being tucked in under her warm duvet in the kind of warmth that a medieval kitchen girl had likely never known.

She shivered again, some of the dream fragments coalescing one more time. Not the young girl on the rocks, but the barely seen face in the waters beyond. Tortured blue-gray eyes, receding into the ocean mists. A watcher.

One who had left Holly's heart galloping like she'd gone for a morning run, and her tears in full working order.

She reached up, bemused, and felt the dampness on her cheeks. Stories had always been able to make her cry, but generally they did it while she was awake. Dreams usually had that haze of sleep that made them not quite so immediate, not quite so real.

This one felt like she'd lived it.

Probably the number of pieces it had borrowed from her life. Love-crazed teenagers and aching legs, a dead mother, and even the weirdly real taste of the cheese that had been the only thing left in her fridge to snack on before bed.

She scowled at her subconscious and the dangerous waters it played in. It could darn well plagiarize a little less next time, and then maybe her dreams would feel like their usual mild entertainment instead of a chapter of her life being lived out in a slightly alternate reality.

The blue-gray eyes swam into Holly's vision again. Disquiet. Unease. Eyes that saw far too much—and a dream whose edges still felt far too real.

Her hand reached out unerringly for the bottle of ibuprofen that always sat by her bed. It was bad enough that her legs bugged her when she was awake—the pain could darn well stay out of her dreams. She grimaced as she poured out two of the small pink tablets and swallowed them dry. Her painkiller intake had gotten too high again, the consequences of too little time for the Pilates exercises that kept her reasonably nimble and too much time sitting in a chair trying to convince the Haversham Institute's powers-that-be that they'd done a good thing by granting her a fellowship.

Maybe it was time to look into a standing desk again. She never felt like her brain worked when it hung out that far above the ground, but it was better than feeling like an eighty-year-old woman on a Saturday morning.

She shivered, still feeling far too connected to an innocent young kitchen girl with moonlight and love in her eyes and the kind of pain in her legs that lanced through Holly even in memory. A message, maybe, that she took the miracle of modern painkillers far too for granted.

Assuming that her subconscious bothered itself with that kind of trivia.

She closed her eyes, the storytelling part of her brain more awake now, calling up details she'd almost let slide away. In that odd way of dreams, she'd seen what Mirena hadn't. The three impossibly beautiful women sitting on rocks in the sea just beyond the girl's line of sight, singing their haunting, yearning melody. And behind them, a ghost in the mists, the almost transparent face of a much older woman.

She didn't look older—she hardly looked older than Mirena herself. But those eyes had seen far too many things. Blue-gray fierceness in a halo of wild brown hair.

Fierceness—and torment.

Holly hummed the opening bars of the song Mirena had heard. Ethereal notes, and ones that tugged on her, even with the very poor early morning rendition. It was music that leaned on her yearning to know the things unseen, to feel the things just beyond what was known and understood.

Things that didn't fit in academic papers, even at the offbeat and independent Haversham Institute. Holly growled and stopped singing, dismissing the music's tug with an annoyed toss of the covers. Mythology and dream interpretation weren't all that far apart, and she didn't want to deal with the messages this dream was clearly trying to sneak in the back door. She'd built a good life, she did good work, and if it involved keeping a leash on her mystical heart sometimes, that was something she'd just have to deal with, no matter what her subconscious might think.

Holly swung her legs out of bed. She was due back at the

Inkspot in a couple of hours, and the list of life minutia she needed to deal with between now and then was long and not very well documented. Time for caffeine.

She didn't have the time to be either innocent or foolish today. Even if the tears on her cheeks thought differently.

HOLLY GRIMACED at the dregs in her coffee cup. Their color was the same as the lashing brown hair that had framed tormented, angry, blue-gray eyes.

So much for banishing the dream ghosts—instead, her night imaginings had grown legs and taken a seat at the breakfast table. Which would have been okay if her nocturnal fantasies had involved a couple of hunky guys and a hot tub on a deserted island, but haunting music and even more haunted eyes weren't exactly cheery fare for the beginning of her weekend.

As Saturday morning breakfasts went, this one was pretty much a dud.

She poked a fork at her freezer-burned toaster waffle. Somewhere in between today's wall-to-wall rehearsals, she needed to get to the grocery store. Toaster waffles were her emergency stash, and the expiration date on these had been dubious at best.

Normally, she enjoyed food gathering—the local market was well stocked, quirky, and great visual fodder for someone who enjoyed watching mythology alive and well in modern times. Love and loss, beauty and treachery, danger and hopeless quests, all roaming the aisles of the Village Foodmart. Most of the key premises of her thesis on the expression of

female sexuality in ancient stories had been formulated somewhere between the neat cereal pyramids and the fresh fruit
display. With the occasional detour to the meat counter,
where Monster worked at his day job. The man made the best
sausage in five counties, which pleased the locals greatly and
made more than one lady take a second glance at the guy
doing the grinding.

Holly just liked his jambalaya brats. Culturally confused,
but yummy as all get-out.

She stuck her fork in the toaster waffle and pushed it
across the table. No way she was going to be able to choke
that down when she had sausages on the brain. Maybe
Monster could be talked into bringing an emergency delivery
to rehearsal.

Or she could skip her need for clean clothes and do a food
run now. She shook her head even as she thought of it. The
Foodmart was true chaos on a Saturday morning, and
rehearsal with Ian and an unsheathed sword was going to be
more than enough of that in her day—she didn't need to
tangle with rampaging toddlers pushing grocery carts too.
Although most of the toddlers at least gave you an adorable
grin after they mowed you down. Ian just figured it was part
of suffering for their art.

Holly sighed and leaned her head back against the wall. *I
see you, bright lady.* Even a determined effort to drive the
tortured eyes away with thoughts of sausage and toddlers
clearly wasn't working. The dream was sticking, and it was
starting to pull on more than just Holly's heartstrings. Her
researcher neurons were coming online as well.

Mythology didn't just happen at the grocery store.

Women singing laments over the water was a pretty iconic

element in at least two oral traditions and three mythological systems she could think of, but her mind very quickly considered and discarded most of them. Those eyes had belonged to a siren, as had the perfect bodies, glittering fishy tails, and tempting lamentations of the trio on the rocks. Sirens or mermaids, depending on your particular mythological leanings and imbibing of the Disney Kool-Aid.

Holly set the feet of her chair back down on the floor and grunted. There was a whole chapter of the book she was writing as part of her fellowship devoted to the disempowerment of women in the movie versions of fairy tales. It was also already written, and not a can of worms she wanted to re-open.

Assuming her brain intended to give her a choice in the matter.

She contemplated the dead toaster waffle, the growling in her belly, and the increasing noise from the bouncing ideas in her head, none of which were shaking off either ghostly eyes or the unease she'd woken up with, and sighed. So much for a chilled-out Saturday morning.

Standing up gingerly, she hobbled over to the architectural wonder of milk crates and salvaged boards that did yeoman's duty as her primary bookshelf, and ran her finger along well-worn spines. It wasn't the drier academic stuff she needed this morning—those authors tended to the stuffy-librarian view of women, especially mostly naked ones. Something told Holly that the blue-gray eyes of her dream wouldn't be overly impressed. Those eyes weren't the kind you pigeonholed or stuffed into nice, neat analytical boxes, and definitely not the kind you dismissed.

Instead, she pulled out a couple of very well-thumbed

titles, *A Complete Guide to Mythological Creatures* and her personal favorite, *Not Everything Is an Allegorical Penis*. She'd met Dr. Shelley Linden, author of the latter—a sharp researcher and very sexy librarian—more than once at conferences now, and the woman was her personal idol. If someone had an opinion on temptresses with fish tails that differed from the mainstream, it would be Dr. Linden.

She popped open *Mythological Creatures* first. It was an excellent basic reference, and Holly liked to know the mainstream opinion before she took a stance against it. Occasionally the mainstream view wasn't entirely crazy, and she was trying to grow out of the tendency to tilt at academic windmills sight unseen.

The short version was more or less what she remembered. Sirens were sex symbols of the dangerous-to-men variety, using songs and various naked body parts to lure unsuspecting innocents to their deaths. Lots of sad storylines, lots of mystery about their origins, and a surprising amount of continuity across cultures on the whole pain-involved-with-having-legs deal.

Holly's thematic Spidey senses tingled. Pain as a metaphor for female choice, or the costs of it. It bore similarities to the biblical stories portraying the pain of childbirth as a punishment for Eve's original sin. Deserved suffering as a gender because one woman had dared to choose. Sometimes myths were about as subtle as sledgehammers, and this wouldn't be the first time the hammer got wielded by cultures trying to keep the fairer sex in their place.

Holly reached for Dr. Linden, who tended to call sledgehammers where she saw them, and grinned as she read the opening lines of the chapter on sirens. *There are a lot of ways we try to dumb down female sexuality or make it less scary. On the surface, the siren archetype is one of the most offensive—but if you look under the hood, this one gets pretty interesting.*

Pay dirt.

She settled in and reached for the toaster waffle. It would have to do, because she definitely wanted at least a quick peek under this particular hood before she poured herself into a corset two sizes too small in order to fulfill male fantasies down at the Inkspot. That activity was going to require focus, and lots of it. Holly needed the blue-gray eyes to go away, and Dr. Linden was the closest thing to a ghostbuster she had on hand.

Like the toaster waffles, it would have to do.

CHAPTER SIX

*H*olly cringed as Ian's sword nearly lopped off her eyelashes. This rehearsal was a nightmare, and she couldn't even blame most of it on the raving lunatic with bad aim who was supposed to be her love interest.

Responsibility for that fell squarely on the imaginary eyes that wouldn't leave her alone. She was totally out of sorts. The disquiet she thought she'd tamed with toaster waffles and Dr. Linden had grown tentacles and spread out under every inch of her too-tight corset. A dream that had no intention of being ignored, and it was walloping her normally unflappable acting skills.

"Take five." Matteo leaned on the edge of the stage and set down his clipboard, which was covered in indecipherable scrawl.

Holly was pretty sure at least half of that would eventually be aimed at her. She'd been a cranky, out-of-tune, mark-missing, line-forgetting, totally unbelievable princess all afternoon, and they hadn't even gotten to the hard parts of the script yet. Opening night was in four days, and Matteo could totally be forgiven for tossing her out the front door and replacing her with the first biddable five-year-old he could find.

She walked over to their very patient director, neatly avoiding two corpses and a cardboard tree branch Ian had accidentally lopped off while declaring his undying love. "I'm really sorry. My focus is shot."

"Yeah, got that," said Matteo dryly. "Nice timing."

Screwing up dress rehearsal was a totally amateur move, even in community theater, and she prided herself on being a pro. "I'll get it together for the second act, I promise."

He eyed her with a mix of agitation and concern. "If you don't, Ian will take your head off with that bleeding weapon of his, and I'll be accessory to murder."

It was way too early in the weekend for their director to be frazzled, even around the edges. This called for emergency measures. "I'll go grab pizza—my treat." Not in her budget, but Holly figured she could probably subsist for the rest of the month on the leftovers in the break room at work. The Haversham Institute hosted enough meetings that pickings were usually pretty good.

Matteo lifted an amused eyebrow. "We're not that far in the crapper."

That might be his opinion. "I am."

"You don't need pizza. You need work." He pointed in the direction of a pile of scenery and props. "Go help wrangle the stage set for the second act, and we'll send around the pizza jar later if you and Ian make it through your big duet without anyone ending up dead."

The man knew how to motivate his people. Holly just

wished he knew how to exorcise a ghost. "I'm hungry now." And she was rapidly developing a theory that a siren wouldn't want to share space with salami breath.

Matteo grinned and waved at the stack of scenery again. "Monster's got pretzels. If you're really nice, he might even share them."

Monster's pretzels were big, chewy, homemade, and accompanied by five-alarm mustard he imported from some undisclosed location in New York. Hot enough to scare away even tortured siren eyes. A decent plan B.

Holly made her way in the direction of the prop master's lair, pondering the disaster that was her focus. Maybe her dreams were onto something deep—a life lesson, or a hidden message, or some pathological bit of her past choosing now to rise up like a zombie and eat her brain.

She'd almost managed to cheer herself up with the idea of zombie dreams when she collided with a hard edge and narrowly avoided bouncing off a concrete wall as she tried to keep herself from a full-blown face-plant.

"Yikes—are you okay?" Warm hands steadied her, and worried brown eyes studied her face like it might belong to a fourteenth-century goddess triptych. "I totally wasn't watching where I was going, my bad."

Holly tried to say something blithe and reassuring, and mostly managed a garbled mumble. Cheeks burning, she tried again. "I wasn't either."

"Sure you're okay?" He still hadn't taken his hands off her shoulders, like he was worried she and the corset might not have their shit together quite yet.

She nodded and searched frantically for something less scatterbrained to say. "I heard Monster brought pretzels."

"Yup." New guy grinned, looking wildly relieved. "I told him I'd work for the princely wage of two pretzels an hour, so long as he throws in extra mustard."

The man must have a stomach of iron. "Have you met his mustard? It makes grown men weep on a regular basis."

He laughed and leaned in close, pitching his words at a whisper. "I know. It's my granny who makes it." He retreated to a more socially standard distance. "I ate it by the spoonful when I was a kid."

He was cute, friendly, in tight with Monster, and he could probably breathe fire—and Holly had to spend the rest of her day dueling with a thirty-eight-year-old father of three with delusions of warrior grandeur. Fate was totally not on her side today. She smiled wryly, tugged at one of the corset ribs that was stabbing her in the gut, and reached for one of the scenery panels she'd managed to run into. "If I help you move heavy things, can I snag half a pretzel?"

He laughed and reached for the other end of the panel. "I've never moved heavy things with a princess. That probably earns you a whole one."

Especially if she didn't run into any more of the things he was carrying. "Done." Holly smiled, feeling a little bit more like herself and a lot less like a pawn of her subconscious.

Until she realized the blue-gray eyes in her head hadn't left —and she had the oddest sense they were pleased.

Which made the knots in her stomach head right back to where they'd started.

HOLLY STEPPED out of a small alleyway that in the daytime

funneled a steady stream of tourists and townspeople toward the river walk that ran behind the theater. By New England standards, it was neither a famous river nor a picturesque one, but like the Inkspot, the town worked with what they had.

Evening rehearsal started up in less than an hour, and she had some serious work to do. Her big monologue scene was up first thing, and Matteo had changed the words on her again two days ago. Tonight was a good time to stop flubbing them, especially after the disaster she'd been all afternoon. This might be community theater, but that wasn't the same thing as amateur comedy hour, and she prided herself on being solid under stress.

Hopefully, pride and two slices of pizza with extra salami would get the job done.

Holly looked up at the night sky and winced. She'd had some vague notion of coming to sit under the moon—there were no uncluttered corners left in the theater, and she'd wanted to clear her head. Instead, she was pretty sure she'd just set herself up to feel like an extra in Mirena's dream, and that was going to land her one monologue away from full actress meltdown.

She resolutely peeled her eyes off the sky. There were things out here to commune with besides the moon. She scrambled down a stretch of slippery, wet embankment, aiming at the small footbridge that spanned the river. And winced some more, because her legs totally weren't up for this kind of abuse after playing dodge-the-sword with Ian all day.

She landed in an ungainly heap at the foot of the railing that led onto the bridge and pulled herself up, muttering very unprincelesslike curses in as many languages as she could remember.

Which lasted about thirty seconds, and then she stopped, feeling entirely ridiculous. Even by the admittedly loose standards of a small New England village, this was weird behavior. Not the kind that required men in white jackets, but not particularly sane, either. And she was totally annoyed that her current state of mind had formed in the warmth and safety of her own bed, tucked under a down comforter that had been with her since childhood.

Not generally the ingredients for a Holly Castas meltdown.

She pulled herself into a standing position and took a tight hold on the railing. No way was she topping off this night with an impromptu dunk in the river. That wasn't fun at any time of year, and given how badly her legs would seize up in the cold waters, she'd probably never make it back out.

She wanted to grace the front page of the *Town Crier* this week, but not as a dead body found by a couple of innocent kids out fishing on Sunday morning. Assuming kids even did that anymore. Rivers around here looked pretty, but they often had murky histories and even murkier industrial sludge embedded in the river bottoms.

Another good reason not to fall in.

Holly watched the dark waters flowing by, their ripples drawing strange, ephemeral shapes as they passed. Not ocean waves—but not entirely different, either, especially with the moonlight glinting off the river's dark progress.

The song that had haunted her all day long rose in her throat, and she hummed it under her breath. It sent shivers up her spine, even without the dream stage props.

Maybe the best way around the craziness was through it.

She hummed louder, and then let the sound climb into a wordless lament. A quiet one—she truly wasn't courting a visit from the men in white jackets. Even at low volume, it pulled on something sharp in her heart.

Her ears could hear that she was leagues away from making a decent siren, but somehow, that didn't seem to matter. She could almost feel ghostly eyes singing counterpoint alongside her, haunting notes that crawled up her skin and sent her heart skittering away from the eerie perfection.

Because no matter how glorious the harmonies were, nothing in Holly wanted to have anything to do with that terrible beauty. And yet, nothing in her knew how to turn away.

The dark shapes in the river shifted, and now she was looking at the face from her dreams. The wild, fierce eyes, windows to a soul who had seen far too much and sang in a way that crawled on Holly's last nerve.

Holly shuddered. She was wide awake this time, and this was way too creepy for words. She pushed herself away from the railing with enough force that she nearly overbalanced the other direction. Stumbling on cold, dysfunctional legs, she headed for the alley she never should have come out of in the first place.

She was going back inside where the air was stale, the walls were old friends, and there was enough leftover hot mustard to get rid of whatever still ailed her.

A show needed to go on tonight—and it wasn't this one.

CHAPTER SEVEN

*D*edra swam to her favorite shallow rock and pillowed her head on its cool surface, tail flicking gently in the waters behind her, and considered what had just happened.

Novelty was very rare in a life as long as hers, but this had been new.

It had hardly been a duet for the ages. The girl had reasonable skills, but she feared what lived inside herself yet—and was perhaps wise enough to fear what lived inside a bitter old siren as well. A thousand years was enough time to fill every note of a song with fierce and terrible longing.

Dedra let a sigh pass out over the shallow rocks as she drank in the echoes of her voice blending with that of another. Inept as the harmonies had been, she could feel her skin soaking in every last drop. It had been a hundred years and more since she'd last sung with her sisters. Cleatris and Sophia had let go together, abandoning a quest worse than futile and damning their blood for the rest of eternity.

Or they would have, had Dedra not chosen to remain.

She reached out and touched the skull that was Sophia's—it had her high, slashing cheekbones, and Dedra sometimes found herself talking to it in the long, dark nights. Or drenching it in scorching fury. It had taken her a very long time to forgive their betrayal.

Their weakness.

Picking up their burden had nearly killed her, but the curse was clear. When one woman stepped up to sing, others of her bloodline were spared. Those who sang well enough joined the sisters in the water—and their voices, the songs of those who had beaten back the curse once, did much to hold it at bay from others of their blood.

She sang for them all. For the daughters of her daughters, and for those of Cleatris and Sophia and all the others who had let go before another sister of their blood could be found. She could not protect every daughter—but she was all that stood between an ancient curse and its eternal, unfettered hunting. She could not be weak, even if her best chance for a new sister in five hundred years was a young woman named after a foolish red berry.

Dedra sighed again. The singing had been barely passable, but the girl had heard it, and showed herself willing to remember it, and that was impressive progress—the kind that required a heart and mind that just might be open enough for what was to come. And there had been a note or two that spoke of readying, even if Holly Castas didn't yet know what she was about to face.

Hearts always knew first, and Dedra knew well that most of them didn't find the bravery to keep listening. This one might, even if she sang on the edge of a polluted, land-bound, infernally cold river.

Dedra's tail swished restlessly in the warm, briny waters she lay in. So much was alien in this modern world, but she understood what her sisters had not. It was the essence that mattered, not the frippery. And while her very bones were offended at the idea of *swimming in waters that had never met so much as a handful of salt, she would willingly walk in the dreams of a girl who spent her days pretending to be a princess with a brain smaller than a pea and spouting silly nonsense onto papers that hardly anyone would ever read.*

Storytellers had been far more respected in her time.

So had princesses.

But this was the best that her blood, diluted over many centuries and far too many years away from salty ocean waters, could give her to work with. And so she would reach out her waning powers to a girl named after a bush and hope that the heart inside the girl had not entirely forgotten what she was.

Or what she could be, if she was willing to claim it. If she was brave enough, and fierce enough, and cruel enough to make the choice.

If she didn't, it would break her anyhow.

Dedra fought the boulders trying to lodge themselves in whatever was left of her heart. Pity wasn't something she could afford to let live inside her, or yearning, or fear. Her sisters had died under their terrible weights.

It was time to push the girl a little. Time to show her more.

Dedra slipped into the water, flicking her strong, battered tail, and dove into the deep. There was fine fishing not too far away. She would swim under the moon and gather her strength.

And then she would walk again in Holly's dreams.

CHAPTER EIGHT

*S*he almost hadn't come.

Mirena slid down the last part of the path to the beach, cursing whatever unnaturally nimble creatures had made a trail so impossible to walk. It surely wasn't goats— they might be climbers enough for such a trek, but they would find her cove utterly uninteresting, devoid as it was of anything tasty to eat.

She patted the small packet at her waist, pleased that it hadn't dislodged during the scramble down. The drier weather had weakened some of her handholds, and the journey had been a precarious one at best.

A sign, perhaps, that she should be at home, tucked into her bedroll with all the other unmarried girls who worked in the big house. It had been a long day, full of early preparations for the midsummer feast. There had been the making of jams and jellies and sweetmeats, turning cheeses, rendering the fats that would become pies and pastries over the days to come. Tomorrow would be more of the same, and the day after that.

She shouldn't have come, but the moon had tugged at her all the long day.

Which was foolish nonsense, really. The moon was no more aware of a mere kitchen girl than she was of a fly buzzing past a blade of grass in the meadow.

Although to hear Mikel tell it, the creeping, crawling, flying things deserved more attention than they got. They certainly got enough of his.

Mirena settled herself in the cool sand, well aware that she was cranky and out of sorts, just like a babe cutting his first teeth. Her man had been gone for most of a fortnight now, off to the city markets with the wagons full of early summer bounty. Most of the goods had been from Narbin's land, where Mikel worked as a laborer, but he'd also added in three small sacks of the herbs and salves the two of them had painstakingly dried and mixed over the winter. Mirena's mother had taught her the making of a salve that eased bone pain, and it fetched a pretty price at the city markets. Enough so that she'd sent Mikel off with her last jars and gone without.

It would be worth it to bring their handfasting that much closer.

She missed him so much. They never got to spend much time together in the warmest months—the hours in the fields were long, and the demands on the workers at the big house were almost as fierce as they picked and preserved and put away for the winter. But always they managed a few minutes together. Sometimes he came in the early morning to help her bring in wood for the kitchen fire, or on occasion she would sneak down to the fields with a loaf of still-warm bread and a bit of cheese deemed not fit for the big house. Cook was in a generous mood these days, with the brigands gone and the Sinchin feeling wealthy enough to have added two more girls to the kitchen.

Mirena reached up a hand to tuck an errant strand of hair behind her ear, and realized her fingers were covered in sand. She looked down, confused, and saw that she'd drawn a picture in the sand. It was an embarrassingly poor rendition of Mikel's face—his ears weren't nearly that big, and his hair wasn't that unkempt even after working in the fields all day.

She rubbed her palm over the childish drawing. Mooning away like the silliest young girl, all because her man had a job to do and had gone off to do it. She should be grateful he wasn't a fighter or a shepherd or anything else that might take him away from the village for months at a time.

Farmers tended to stay close to home, and they tended to stay safe. It wasn't that long ago that Lindeen's man had been pierced through on a late spring hunt. The healers said he might walk again, but that was the best they could hope for. Lindeen's eyes had been full of fear ever since. Not a surprise—she had four small mouths to feed, and her man had been one of the village's best providers.

Even in midsummer, the specter of hunger was never that far away.

Mirena breathed in deeply of the smell of the sea. Her heart was restless tonight, unsettled and feeding strength to worries where none was needed. She turned her ears to the waves, listening for the sound of the music that always came. Nothing yet. Sometimes the singing started even as she arrived. Sometimes she sat for hours, waiting, shivering.

There would be no shivering tonight. The air was warm, with not even a hint of chill. She reached for the food packet at her waist. Perhaps she would have a picnic in the moon-light and dream of Mikel's return. It shouldn't be long now—even with time to make the full rounds of the city, the market wagons were almost never gone longer than a fortnight. The fields needed their farmers back. At this time of year, no hands could be spared any longer, not if they wanted to eat through the winter.

Her heart heard it before her ears did. The faint strains of the eerie, sad music that shouldn't have been anything she wanted to hear, but somehow was.

Mirena breathed in again as it started to ease the pain in her legs. Whatever magic this was, she had long since lost the will to question it. Even Mikel wouldn't understand her need to come, but he didn't know what it was to live with your trai-torous insides stabbing you every hour of the day and night. Only some of the old people of the village understood that kind of pain, and they could comfort themselves with the knowing that their lives drew to an end.

She shook her head and made herself take a big bite of the buttered bread she'd just unwrapped. It was a hard-earned treat. She'd scraped every last bit from the churning barrel, and it was salty, sweet goodness—not something that should feed this kind of bitter melancholy. Her legs weren't so bad at this time of year. The warmth of summer eased them some, and the gardens had herbs to spare for the teas that brought her some relief.

The song was strong tonight. She chewed, letting the sweet, soft butter melt in her mouth, and listened to the various sounds of the music, trying to pick out the different voices. Her ear wasn't trained, but she could hear a lighter voice, and one that felt weighted down with all the sorrows that had ever been.

Mirena peered out into the distance as she always did, looking for the singers.

Mikel would laugh if she told him that part. Squinting into the dark, looking for ghosts.

He could never know of this. It wasn't safe and it wasn't sensible, and she knew for a certainty that it wasn't a thing that would rest easy in his steadfast, solid heart. He would worry for her, and he might even try to forbid it, as some of the men of the village did with their women.

She smiled a little into the dark. Probably not. It wasn't in Mikel to force anything, even the small plants he tended. His music, were he to sing it, would be a song of gentle, steady warmth.

The heavy voice, the one with all the sorrows, grew stronger.

Mirena leaned forward, her heart beating faster in her chest. Tonight was different. Sadder. Harsher.

She shouldn't have come.

Her eyes caught the ripples in the water first. The lines that didn't move quite as water moved, the shadows that cut through waves and changed their shape.

She peered harder into the dark, the bread in her mouth grown dry and hard to swallow.

The lines made their way toward a shallow gathering of rocks not far from the beach. Sunning rocks, if only there were any sun. Mirena watched, dazed and frozen, as first one shadow and then another made its way up out of the water.

She gasped as the first turned her face up into the moonlight. A woman, but not a mortal one—of that, Mirena's eyes were entirely sure. Visage and cheekbones sharp as daggers, mouth open and rending the air with her terrible song.

This was the one who sorrowed.

Mirena wondered if perhaps she had fallen on the climb down after all, and these were creatures of the dead come to collect her.

Except they didn't look dead. They looked so very real in their glistening nakedness and their scaly tails, and so very full of power.

She would have thought them sea serpents but for their song. The last bits of bread in her mouth turned to dust. She knew what they were now—the fishermen from the next village over spoke of them at festivals when they got deep into the drinking barrels.

Sirens. Cursed creatures, half woman, half fish, who called good men to their deaths.

She'd never heard of them singing to a woman.

Mirena cowered, unable to take her eyes off the three glistening creatures on the rocks. Their song was impossibly beautiful and utterly inhuman. It made her heart want to run for the farthest reaches of the plains and never look on the ocean waters again.

And it made her want to swim to the rocks and join them forever.

They had come for her—she knew that without a doubt, even as she felt her limbs shivering in terror.

Their singing gentled some. The highest voice, the one that knew of some happiness, sang wordless notes of calm to Mirena's spirit.

Her limbs stilled, but now terror stalked her very soul.

The three sirens put their heads together for a moment,

and then the one in the middle slid into the water and swam forward, as graceful and sinuous as the small snakes that played in the field grasses, and far more dangerous. When she reached the shallow waters, she stood, clad only in a sheer shawl and a couple tendrils of seaweed that did more to reveal than they did to hide.

Mirena knew she was gaping like a toddler at her first Midwinter's Night.

"Come now, surely you've seen a naked body before." The voice was husky and almost creaky, like it very rarely got used.

Mirena scrambled for something to say, even as fear nearly swallowed her whole. "You have legs."

"It was either that or make you swim to us." The siren raised one shoulder in a careless shrug. "It's warm tonight, so I came to you." She folded her legs elegantly and perched on the edge of Mirena's rock, skin glistening in the moonlight. "Your legs pain you."

Not on this night. Not anymore. "They often do. It afflicted my mother as well." Perhaps if she kept talking, they wouldn't kill her.

The siren's smile was somehow sad. "It afflicts all the women of our blood who walk the land."

Mirena's ability to think clearly skittered off into the dark shadows. She could not possibly be related to this creature of the terrible eyes and inhuman song.

"My blood runs in you, daughter. As does the ancient curse that holds us bondage."

"A curse?" Mirena hadn't known her voice could squeak like a mouse.

"Its beginnings aren't known." The siren picked up a small

handful of sand and let it trail through her fingers. "I am Kleia. I was a maiden once, just as you are. In love, and nearly drunk with the power of it."

It wasn't power. "He makes me happy." She squeezed her eyes shut, desperately afraid that she would never see Mikel's kind face again. No one who had ever seen a siren up this close had lived to tell the tale, she was sure of it. Even the drinking barrel didn't forget a story such as that.

"I am sorry." The weight of all the sorrows of the world landed back in Kleia's voice.

Mirena looked up and found herself swimming in the harsh compassion in the siren's green eyes.

"If it were within my power to spare you this, I would." The creature looked as if she meant it. Then her face hardened, and bitterness flooded her eyes. "But in this, I can offer you no more shield than a puny grain of sand."

Fear slammed back into Mirena's chest. A curse to which this being bowed must be terrible indeed.

The siren reached around her neck and took hold of a pendant nestled between her naked breasts. She lifted it over her head and held it out on her palm. "This is for you. You face a terrible choice, daughter of my blood. One that has been faced by those of our line for millennia."

This wasn't possible. "I'm only a kitchen girl."

"The curse cares only for the power inside you." Sad, bitter tears stained every word, even though the siren's eyes were dry. "You have a great capacity for love, and that has condemned you."

She shouldn't have come. "I don't know what you mean."

"You love a man." The words had suddenly taken on the

formal weight of ritual. Of prophecy. "You carry siren blood in your veins. You must use it now to save his life."

Mirena hadn't thought it was possible to be any more afraid. She'd been wrong. She felt the shudders racking her. "Don't hurt Mikel, please."

"It isn't I who seeks his life. It is the curse." The siren's gaze was remote now, seeing something beyond the cove, beyond the waters, beyond time. Then her eyes snapped back to Mirena's, and for just a moment, fire glowed in them. "Sing, and he will live. Don't sing, and he will die. Sing well enough, and you will become one of us."

She was only a kitchen girl. "I don't know how to sing."

"You know how to love, and that is all you need to know." The siren was gliding back toward the water. "Come the next time the moon is full and sing your love out over the water— it will be most powerful then. Give your man his life. We will be waiting."

Mirena stared, horrified and transfixed.

She shouldn't have come.

Her body shook with one last shudder, and then she felt something settle around her neck. Her hand reached up reflexively and closed around a cold, wet form.

The siren's pendant. It could be nothing else.

Fury rose up, a hot, rebellious wave of it. Mirena yanked the leather thong over her head and hurled it out into the waters as hard and as far as she could.

And watched, helpless and heartsick, as a wave pushed it right back up onto the beach.

CHAPTER NINE

*H*olly yanked into consciousness, sucking for air, grabbing for the writhing thing around her neck that was trying to steal her life—and froze, not even daring to blink, as two things became blindingly obvious.

This was her room, with the lights still on, the folk rock still blaring from her iPod, and the old movie posters wallpapering her ceiling.

Unmistakably her room. Just as the thing around her neck was almost certainly the pendant that should still be decorating the African mask in her office.

And it was wet.

It was that last part that had Holly's storyteller heart reeling and her rational brain gibbering in terror in the corner.

Slowly, feeling as ephemeral, fragile, and nonsensical as a spider web of spun glass, she slid an arm behind her back and pushed up to sitting. That didn't help with the dizziness any, or the rampaging nausea, but it did let her take stock of the alternate reality she'd apparently beamed into.

It looked strangely like the old one. Half a slice of pizza congealed on her desk by the iPod, and the haphazard pattern of socks, t-shirts, and stray tissues suggested that she hadn't managed to either fully undress or fully clean the stage makeup off her face before she'd passed out on her bed.

She reached a ginger fingertip to her face and groaned. Definitely still gunked, and that was enough to give anyone nightmares.

Wincing, she wiggled her toes, flexed her calves. And raised a surprised eyebrow. Legs in fairly good working order, which they shouldn't have been after a long day of gliding like a princess while dodging swords, overeager costume people, and errant stage props. She eyed the ibuprofen bottle warily—maybe she'd finally managed to overdose.

A drip of water landed on her naked thigh.

Holly shivered, and not from her lack of pajama bottoms. With dread a nasty, pulsing golf ball in her throat, she reached up to her neck and lifted the damp pendant over her head.

It was soaking wet, particularly the leather thong. Briny, salty wet.

And her hair smelled like the sea.

The siren hadn't been speaking only to Mirena. Her words had felt personal—so deeply, impossibly personal. Holly's rational brain could scream all it wanted, but her storyteller heart was trembling right alongside that of a medieval kitchen girl.

She threw the pendant, whimpering as it barely made it as far as the half-eaten pizza.

This was getting old, really fast.

CHAPTER TEN

$\mathcal{H}$olly stepped in the open door of the Foodmart, still dripping with sweat, and inhaled the pervasive smell of baked goods and the sharp sweetness of the strawberry display right inside the front door. How they got strawberries that red in real life was anyone's guess, but judging by the holes in the display, she wasn't the first person today who would be going home with some.

She leaned over to set a carton in the wheeled basket that was the safest way to navigate the Foodmart's narrow aisles, and groaned as she pushed back up to standing. She had a whole lot of muscles that were already warning her they intended to take their revenge, and soon. Hopefully, she could stave off that revenge with a preemptive strike. Ninety minutes of turning herself into a gibbering puddle of Pilates sweat had totally earned her a frying pan full of sausages and some crispy noodles to go with them.

With an on-the-fly addition of strawberries and whipped cream for dessert.

That was the plan, assuming her legs managed to keep working long enough to get to the meat counter. Holly walked gingerly, fairly certain it would cause a scene if she collapsed in the middle of the fresh produce. The Pilates advanced class probably hadn't been a smart idea, given that she'd missed at least three weeks and Desirée never took pity on anyone, even on a Sunday morning.

But she'd had a dream to exorcise, and somewhere in the middle of the third set of abdominal curls, even siren eyes hadn't been able to swim their way through the shrieking protests of core muscles that had spent way too much time locked in a corset.

Holly grabbed an apple on her way out of produce and took a bite. At least her jaw muscles still felt relatively perky. A quick detour through dairy for a carton of whipping cream and she'd be ready to visit Monster and see what he'd been grinding up in the dark hours.

Possibly actors, given the way rehearsals had gone yesterday.

"Hey."

The voice was friendly as it reached for a carton of milk over her left shoulder.

Holly glanced up and caught some of the face it belonged to. "Hey, yourself." She searched her mind frantically for a name, and concluded that she'd somehow managed not to get one.

"Jamie." He shifted the milk to his left hand and held out his right. "I'm pretty sure I forgot to introduce myself while I was mowing you over with scenery panels yesterday."

He hadn't been the one doing the mowing, but she wasn't going to argue with a first-class distraction. "I'm Holly."

He smiled and reached for a carton of eggs, and then grimaced and put them back.

Holly held out her hand. "If you don't need those, I do." Fried eggs and toast were her standard weekday morning breakfast, and right now the only part of that feast that inhabited her kitchen was the fork.

He handed the rejected carton her direction. "Sorry, I'm an egg snob. I built my girls a new house and they're still getting used to the place, so supplies are low, but it pains me to buy supermarket eggs."

She felt a sudden bizarre need to defend the Foodmart. "They usually carry local eggs except for in the dead of winter —they're really good."

His smile was much bigger this time. "They're mine. Thanks for buying them."

"You're an egg farmer?"

"Amongst other things. I grow organic greens and veggies for the restaurants around here, and I keep chickens to chase my bug population." He surveyed the cheeses and picked something French and yummy.

Holly sighed and picked something American and cheap. "You're the guy who sends the micro greens to the Burger Shack, right?" Their paleoburger was the highlight of her dining week when she could afford it.

This time he laughed. "Are you one of the Haversham Institute people? You guys eat a lot of greens."

Not a surprise—the Burger Shack was right across the street from the sprawling building that served as Haversham's main campus. "Guilty. My best friend singlehandedly consumes your entire mushroom crop." Jade had a thing for spores and fungi, edible and otherwise.

"Tell her the first batch of shiitakes lands next week."

She'd be stalking the Burger Shack at the crack of dawn. "I'll let her know." Holly surveyed her rolling basket, which had mysteriously filled itself halfway up. She added a pint of whipping cream to the top of the pile. "I need to pay a visit to Monster, and then I think my work here is done."

Jamie patted a messenger bag hanging off his shoulder. "I'll join you—I've got secret ingredients for his sausages."

That would explain the green stuff that occasionally showed up in her frying pan. "Is it your fault that he puts kale in with perfectly good ground turkey?"

He glanced at her, amused. "You don't like kale? Weirdo."

Holly snickered, mostly under her breath. "Says the guy who murders fingernail-sized plants and feeds their corpses to the unsuspecting populace."

This time he full-on laughed, and when he did, something warm and bright turned over in her belly. First-class distraction, indeed. They swung companionably toward the back of the store, dragging their respective wheeled baskets.

Monster saw them coming and waved from behind the meat counter. "I'm not sure if it's safe for the two of you to be hanging out together."

Holly shrugged. "You didn't protest when we moved scenery panels yesterday."

"Self-preservation." He was already digging out the sausages she liked best. "I know better than to argue with a dame in laces and a hoop skirt."

Jamie tracked the conversation, still looking amused. "I'll take six of the turkey sausages with the murdered kale."

"Can't." Monster didn't look very sorry. "Holly's getting the last ones. She never leaves enough for anyone else."

Jamie looked at Holly, eyebrows raised.

Busted. She shot Monster a mostly fake dirty look and shrugged. "Little dead green bodies—what's not to like?"

An old lady with purple-rinsed hair shot her a concerned look and backed up several paces.

"Quit scaring the natives," said Monster under his breath, before giving the worried customer his best cleaver-wielding-softie smile. "What can I get for you this morning, Mildred?"

It turned out she wanted kale and turkey sausages too. Holly clutched her package of them and backed away, fighting off an attack of the giggles. Jamie dropped a paper bag on top of the meat counter and joined her, and they scurried away like two guilty accomplices.

She grabbed a can of baked beans as they escaped via the canned goods aisle. No point wasting what might be her only chance this week to repair the empty state of her cupboards.

And then they were at the end of the aisle, the checkout lines were three feet away, and they'd suddenly hit the awkward part of grocery-store conversations where someone still needed tomatoes and nobody was exactly sure how to part ways. Holly briefly considered inviting Jamie over for sausages and strawberries, but rapidly discarded the idea. She probably wasn't that bold, and her apartment definitely wasn't that clean.

He laid a casual hand over hers on the shopping basket. "See you at rehearsal on Tuesday?"

It was probably stupid to feel relieved that seeing him again was going to be that easy. "Monster's reeled you in, has he?"

Jamie flashed his captivating smile. "He muttered something about final runs and crazy theater people."

It was the last rehearsal before they'd have an audience. Crazy was a nice, polite word for how the Inkspot was going to be on Tuesday night. "However many pretzels he's paying you, it's probably not enough."

His eyes gleamed. "I'll consider myself warned."

Anybody who could handle bug-hunting chickens and spinach murder could probably cope with a little theater insanity. Holly turned away, feeling a little awkward and a little interested and just generally enjoying the buzz of the encounter.

And ran headlong into the eyes that had been watching over her shoulder.

Blue-gray ones nobody else could see.

The nasty, snaking tension of the early morning rushed back into the space she'd just worked for hours to clear. Holly cursed and refused to consider what it all meant, at least until she'd made it out of the Foodmart and back into the questionable comfort of her own space. If she was going crazy, she could at least do it in private.

She dragged her basket grimly away from the cute guy and in the direction of the shortest checkout line. She wanted sausages, strawberries, and a smart pair of ears, probably in that order.

It was time to figure out what to do with her ghostly stalker.

CHAPTER ELEVEN

*H*olly had never been more glad to see her best friend, even without the carton of Chocolate Death gelato teetering perilously on the stack of well-thumbed paperbacks in Jade's hands. All the comfort things. She reached for the frozen goods first. "You're a goddess in shining armor."

"Do those exist?" Jade maneuvered through the door and set the books down on the small thrift-store table that served as the apartment's general dump zone.

"They do now." Holly resisted the urge to cuddle the gelato and headed for the kitchen. "You want a bowl?"

Jade raised a very noisy eyebrow. "Tell the nice alien people that you look like my friend Holly, but they blew it on the brain replication."

That was a definite no on the bowl. Holly pulled out the last two clean spoons left in the drawer and sighed—someone needed to invent a machine that washed dishes and laundry at the same time. "I think I'd rather be dealing with alien people."

Jade's eyes got darker and a lot more focused. "Are you in trouble?"

Holly had no idea. "If I am, it's not any of the usual kinds."

That got an amused look, even through the worry. "Why am I not surprised?"

Because her best friend had a really smart brain behind those piecing green eyes. "I'm getting predictable in my old age?"

Jade took a spoon and herded them in the direction of the lumpy sofa that served as sloth central, spare bed, and occasional therapy couch. "It's some ungodly hour on Sunday morning. Use small words."

It was practically noon, but the heir to the Gleason throne had never been an early riser. And Holly wasn't sure she had a lot of words, of the big or small variety. Even a monster spoonful of Chocolate Death gelato wasn't helping her figure out where to start this particular tale of the bizarre. "You consider yourself pretty rational, right?"

"Uh, oh." Jade's spoonful was slightly more ladylike, probably because her eyes were busy drilling a hole into Holly's head.

"You're a data geek and a scientist in cool clothing, admit it."

More silent spoonfuls of gelato and worried looks.

Holly sighed. "I had a really strange experience. I thought it was a dream, but it happened again, and now I think that maybe it wasn't, and I need you to keep that sane, future-ruler-of-the-corporate-world head on your shoulders while I tell you what happened."

"That's a very frightening opening monologue," said Jade, her spoon paused in midair. "Care to give me the short version so I don't die of a chocolate overdose while I wait for you to get to the good stuff?"

Holly was pretty sure the two of them had spent the last decade conclusively proving chocolate overdose wasn't possible, but she didn't want to torture her Sunday-morning support. "The first weird dream was two nights ago."

Jade assumed her psychoanalyst position on the couch. "This correlates with you running around for hours in a princess gown that was originally designed for a fifteen-year-old stick, right?"

Trust the scientist to remember all the data points. "I'm pretty sure this isn't related to lack of oxygen." Holly sighed—the version of this story that started at the beginning was a long one, and Jade had made a reasonable request. Maybe it was better to tell this one from the other end. Holly reached over to the side table and held out her pendant. "Smell it." The leather thong was almost dry, but it still carried the scent of its swim in the sea.

Jade leaned over to sniff and then fingered the pendant, eyebrows raised. "You raided the office for snacks and jewelry and then you went skinny dipping with a hot guy in the sea-salt baths at the spa?"

Holly had never so much as set foot in the spa, but trust Jade to know where the nearest salt water was. "None of the above. I left the pendant at the office on Friday. This morning, I woke up with it around my neck. It and my hair were both wet. With salt water."

She'd washed her hair with half a bottle of shampoo since then, but her nose still thought it could smell the brine.

Jade regarded the pendant a lot more suspiciously now. "That's creepy."

It did something warm to her insides that her best friend's instincts were to suspect the jewelry, and not Holly's sanity. "I could totally be suffering from oxygen-deprived hallucinations."

Jade sniffed the pendant. "If you are, it's a pretty over-the-top one, complete with very realistic special effects."

A scientist with a really flexible mind. "You believe me."

Jade leaned back. "I believe this is important, and that's all I really need to know for sure." She handed back the pendant. "Okay, I think it's safe for you to start at the beginning now."

Holly's lips twitched at the general bossiness of those words. "Minions in fancy suits will cower in your office one day."

Nothing moved except for one of Jade's highly communicative eyebrows.

Which more or less proved the point. "I had a dream Friday night. One of those ones where you're the person in the dream and the watcher and the narrator all at once."

Jade grinned. "Did it involve hot girls and a lot of chocolate sauce?"

That patented mix of bossy and irreverent was exactly the kind of steadying the doctor had ordered. Holly handed over the rest of the gelato. "No chocolate sauce, but there were hot girls."

Green eyes sparked with laughter. "You could have led with that part."

"They were in the second dream. Sirens, I think, singing to this girl, Mirena, who was sitting on the beach." Holly filled in enough of the backstory to sketch out the important outlines. "And then they told her about this weird curse and that she was the next in line and gave her this terrible choice.

Either she has to sing and become one of them, or Mikel will die."

Jade's eyes weren't amused anymore. "So she loses him either way? That's a pretty sucky curse."

Holly could still feel Mirena's stuttering horror. "She tried not to believe them. She didn't want to."

"Hey." Her best friend leaned forward, hands reaching out to comfort. "This one really got to you, huh?"

It had—she could feel the tears threatening again, even after half a container of chocolate therapy. "She's had a pretty hard life and he's this strong, sexy, farmer type, and all she wants is a simple and good thirty years with him, you know? And now it feels like all she has is tragedies to choose from." Holly sucked in a breath as a rivulet of tears managed to escape down her cheek. "I could feel myself as her, like all the hope in my world had just started circling the drain."

Jade's thumb wiped the tears away. "What's going on that I don't know about, girlfriend?"

Holly shook her head, not understanding. "What?"

"We dream for the same reason as we read stories—to work shit out for ourselves. So if you've got this despondent stuff going on, I feel like I've missed something."

Holly frowned. None of this fit her life at all, at least not the current version. "That's just it—I don't think this is my subconscious at work."

Jade's very expressive eyebrow did its thing again.

Holly held up her still-damp pendant. "Salt water, remember?"

"Good point." The heir to the Gleason throne nodded slowly. "Then you don't have a dream, maybe. You have a mystery."

Or a possible mental health disorder. Holly was deeply grateful that wasn't her best friend's first hypothesis. "I'm not sure what I have." But whatever it was, it felt better that she didn't have it alone. She reached her spoon toward the half-empty carton of Chocolate Death. "Let's find a bad movie to watch with the rest of this. We can let my subconscious work out its angst while the rest of me eats popcorn and forgets to do the laundry."

One of the very best things about Jade was her ability to shift gears at the speed of light. "Suits me. Thriller, classic, or trashy romance?"

Those were all far too likely to head into archetypes that would remind her of blue-gray eyes and a distraught kitchen girl. "Godzilla marathon. In Japanese."

There wasn't much farther you could get from blue-gray eyes than that.

CHAPTER TWELVE

*M*irena ducked under the outstretched arms of the other pairs of dancers and reached for the hand of her partner, huffing for breath as she did so. The fiddler must be getting tired, but he hadn't slowed down his beat all the long night—if anything, it felt like he was getting faster. Maybe something to do with being Ima's brother. The handfasted couple hadn't sat down all evening either, and Ima's homely face shone brighter than anyone else's in the lights of the candle lanterns, the stars, and the smiles of the man she had just joined with.

Burk was one of Mikel's friends, a short, stout, taciturn man who rarely smiled, and to the best of anyone's knowledge, had never danced. Ima had cured him of that two beats into the fiddler's first tune. Apparently, Burk already knew better than to tangle with Ima when she had an idea in her head. When a woman spent her days making stubborn mules mind, a mere man was nothing to bend to her will.

Not that there had been much need tonight. Burk still

wasn't doing much that resembled dancing, but he was shuffling around the meadow in approximately the right patterns, and doing it with the kind of stolid joy on his face that would have melted far harder hearts than anyone in the village possessed. Happiness wasn't all that easy to come by, and people here knew enough to treasure it when it landed. A warm night and a midsummer festival were far more reasons than anyone needed to put on their finest and find the merriment in their steps.

Mirena caught sight of Mikel as she sashayed up the side of the dancers, standing quietly under a tree with several of the men he labored with. Discussing crops, most likely, or working out if they'd enough stores set away to feel comfort through the winter just yet. For her man, that would bring fierce lightness to his heart. He was a provider, one who bloomed in the knowing that his family and his friends and his village would have enough to eat. She would let him stand under the tree a bit longer, and then she'd entice him back out to dance.

They would follow in the happy footsteps of Burk and Ima this night, and hope to be the handfasted couple dancing at the next festival. Their time was coming, she could feel it in her bones.

Mirena took advantage of a momentary break in the music to bid her dance partner goodbye. She made her way to the edge of the meadow, beyond the dancers and the ring of lanterns lighting their steps, and into the shadows and the chatter. Time to find herself a mug of something cool to drink —goodness knows they'd mixed up enough in the kitchens to quench the thirst of the village a dozen times over.

She smiled as Ima's happy laughter brushed by her ear.

Soon, this would be her future. She would not believe the words of wraiths that came to her in waking dreams, no matter how desperately they'd made her heart quiver. Songs didn't keep men alive—and songs unsung didn't send them to their deaths.

The pendant around her neck seemed to shiver.

Mirena wanted nothing more than to hurl it into the darkest night, but resisted. Someone would surely notice, and by now she knew that there was nothing she could do to escape the simple length of leather and its white tear-shaped pearl.

She'd tried. She'd run from the cove and the full moon and the terrible singing, leaving the pendant lying in the sand. And woken up the next morning with it around her neck.

For six frantic days, she'd found new places to leave it. Down a well early one morning, and then up on a high rafter in the attic of the big house, the doing of which had nearly caused her to break her neck. After that, she'd tried leaving the cursed thing near a tree full of crows well known for collecting pretties and treasures. Each morning, she'd woken up to the pendant's cool, chiding presence back around her neck.

Mirena accepted a cup of chilled spring water from Girelle, the newest of the house staff and still quite shy. She nodded approvingly at the girl's soft curtsy, which would please the villagers well, and moved into the shadows, feeling suddenly adrift.

She had been Girelle once, full of the hope and excitement of her new status in the big house, dreaming of a future both simple and unimaginative, but warming to her young heart nonetheless. She'd spent six years leaning into the sometimes harsh realities of her new life and finding her place in it. And now she felt entirely alone, sliced out of the fabric of what was hers and left standing on the edges, watching enviously as the dancers twirled by.

She closed her eyes. This was what they were trying to take from her, those creatures at the cove. Whatever evil trickery they were up to, she must not let it take possession of her mind, claw its way into her heart. She'd seen the healers working often enough to know that a person could make themselves sick or well by nothing more than the power of what they chose to believe.

She would not give the three of the cove such power. The pendant could stay if it must. It was a bauble, nothing more— and not a terribly pretty one at that.

"There you are." Mikel's low voice rumbled into the shadows, his eyes seeking hers in the darkness. He stood directly underneath one of the hanging chains of wildflowers the young girls of the village had strung for the trees, holding a candle lantern in his hand. Surrounded by warm breezes and flowers and gaiety, he resembled one of the earth gods of old, risen up from the richness and the strength of the land itself.

Mirena shook her head, smiling. Always, he tempted her head to such foolishness, leaving her feeling no older or wiser than young Girelle. "I've been dancing all night, unlike some people I know."

He ducked his head, a little bashful. "I'm sorry. We got to talking about the turnip planting in Narbin's far field."

If that was going to bother her, she'd picked the wrong man to love, but there was no point in letting him know that. "Well, at least I know my competition, then." She batted her eyelashes at him like the most wanton maiden. "What must I do to drag you away from the fascination of turnips, my love?"

This time, the bashfulness rose all the way up into his cheeks. "Miri—"

He was the only one who ever called her that, and it cut through any desire she had to tease him about turnips. She moved closer and slid her fingers into his large, warm hand. Words weren't his strength, and she wouldn't use hers to back him into a corner she didn't even want him to be in. He had done no wrong this night. "It's no matter, truly. Let's go see if we can find a pasty or two." The kitchen had made hundreds, savory and sweet both, but they always went quickly. Appetites ran high at this time of year.

Mikel shook his head, eyes gleaming, and took her other hand in his, swinging her into the dancers and nearly lifting her off her feet.

Apparently, he had decided it was time to dance.

Mirena shook her hair behind her, laughing, and joined the rhythm of the music and the flying feet around them. Her legs would pain her in the morning, but for the length of this night, she would choose to forget that happiness came with a price.

It took the man partnering her, with a slow smile stuck on his face, a little longer to get up to speed than most, and his feet would never be the lightest or the fastest, but she imagined that the earth felt his steps and welcomed them. The land knew that Mikel of Innstel danced here. She flitted into his side and then back out again, a honeybee romancing the sturdiest of flowers.

Tonight, she wanted the earth to know of her too.

HOLLY WOKE UP, heart hammering in her throat.

The handfasting had been beautiful, dreamy and romantic as seen through Mirena's eyes, full of simple, fertile hope. One of the happier rituals of an earlier time when life and death were attendant parts of everyday experience.

She squinted against the early morning sun streaming in the windows and tried to swallow her sense of impending dread. The dream had been the kind of interlude that always came in stories right before Voldemort showed up or Pa nearly got killed or the bad guys came for Frodo's ring. If she'd been analyzing this storyline for one of her papers, she would have pointed to the narrative power of such a juxtapositioning of hope with its eventual betrayal.

Instead, she could only sit and clutch the pendant around her neck.

Because Mikel had worn Jamie's face.

And this time, her pendant smelled like fresh flowers.

CHAPTER THIRTEEN

*H*olly looked at the pile of books on her desk and shook her head. None of this was related to the papers she was supposed to be writing.

Her self-assigned reading wasn't *Mythological Creatures* or *Allegorical Penises* this time, either. Dream interpretation, abnormal psychology, stress management—basically a deep search for something more rational to tangle with than an ancient curse that had somehow decided to walk out of her dreams and invade her life. It was an alternative explanation she was seeking, and her undergraduate psych degree had helpfully offered up plenty of potential candidates.

She reached for the book on the top of the pile and sighed. It was never a good Monday when discovering you had a mental health issue would be considered a good outcome.

"Uh, oh." The voice from the doorway sounded cautious, very curious, and short on caffeine.

Holly looked up at the concerned eyes of her best friend and the two monster coffee mugs in her hands, and felt the little bit of spine she'd managed to grow since she'd woken up slither off someplace to die.

Jade was at her desk in an instant. "Honey, what happened?"

"Dream number three."

Small, strong hands wrapped hers around a steaming mug of coffee. "Drink and talk, girlfriend."

Holly wasn't at all sure caffeine was going to help her nerves, but that was a heresy she didn't have the energy to preach this morning. "It was mostly a happy dream. Some kind of summer festival. Folk dancing, lots of food and drink, pretty flowers."

"You aren't hitting the books this morning over flowers. This was your kitchen girl, I assume?"

"Yeah." Daring to be happy, and somehow that made it worse.

"And the creepy siren ladies?"

"They weren't in this one, except indirectly."

Jade sat, eyes grim, waiting for the punch line.

Holly wished she had one to deliver. "Nothing happened, exactly. It's just a feeling, like when they play the scary music in the horror flick right before someone dies."

A long, thoughtful slurp of coffee. "You know, there are studies showing that soldiers in battle often know when they're about to die."

Trust a woman who played with catapults in her spare time to know something like that. "That's comforting."

"There are energies to this stuff, that's all I'm saying."

There was certainly something.

Her best friend leaned over and scanned the spines of the book pile on Holly's desk. When she looked back up, her eyes were full of concern again—and disapproval. "You're researching what might be wrong with you?"

It had felt comforting pulling together a stack of books. "Knowledge is power, right?" That was pretty much axiomatic in the hallowed halls of the Haversham Institute.

"Sometimes." Jade didn't look any less concerned. "I have a cousin who Googles her symptoms every time she gets sick. The answer is always cancer or a brain tumor."

"Okay, knowledge is power for everyone except for your cousin."

One of those small, inconsequential pauses between best friends that both of them knew was loaded.

Holly took a deep breath and said the part that had her entirely freaked out. "Mikel had Jamie's face."

Jade blinked. "Who is Jamie?"

It was Holly's turn to blink. "You spent ten hours at my place yesterday watching Godzilla movies and eating your body weight in chocolate gelato and I never mentioned the cute guy at the grocery store?" Major friend fail—and a sign of just how wonky the last few days had been.

The future ruler of the corporate world took a long sip of coffee, eyes twinkling. "This story just took a major turn for the better."

Not so much. Holly filled her in on the sexy farmer Monster had recruited to schlep scenery panels, and their encounter at the Foodmart.

"Clearly, I need to grocery shop more often." Jade raised an eyebrow. "Does he make your chakras tingle?"

Holly had no plans to talk about anything that tingled. "Is that even a thing?"

"Someone on Facebook said it was, about an hour ago. It's gone viral. There are cute kittens involved."

There always were. The mythology of this generation had some seriously weird forms of expression, mostly cute and furry. "I hardly know him, but I like him so far."

"So do your dreams, apparently." Jade's face was still casual, but her eyes had shifted into business mode.

The little bit of normal that had been working its way back into Holly's Monday morning fled. "Yeah. That part's totally creepy."

Jade sat quietly for a moment. "That part could just be your subconscious." She ran a finger down the book spines and stopped at one on dream interpretation. "This guy talks about how we process the events of our lives in dreams and borrow the faces of people we know to be the dream actors."

Holly gave her friend a look. "Have you read everything?"

"Yes. That's what happens when you take three years to decide on your major." Jade had pulled out the book in question, which wasn't the easiest maneuver ever, given that it had been near the bottom of the stack, and turned to the table of contents. Then she stopped, looked up, and put the book down on the desk. "What?"

"You're taking this seriously." Somehow, that felt deeply important—and deeply scary. "I keep hoping it's just a dream." The garden-variety kind that went away if you stuck your head in the sand for long enough.

"So if it's just a dream, you get to ignore it?" Jade looked like a stern schoolteacher.

Clearly, that wasn't the right answer. "Uh—no?"

"Look. Either this is real, your pendant somehow made its way from the African ladies to your bed, you woke up wet and smelling like seaweed, and there's some seriously strange shit going on..." Her best friend kept right on rolling like those were totally reasonable words to say on a Monday morning. "Or you're having some very realistic dreams that are affecting you deeply, to the point that maybe you're hallucinating or teleporting things."

Holly wasn't at all fond of either of those explanations.

"Either way, you need to take this seriously."

Holly gestured at the pile of books on her desk. "I'm trying."

"That's your brain trying. You need to get the rest of Holly Castas on the job."

That was easier said than done. "She's busy playing a whiny princess." Badly, thanks to the whole siren-haunting deal.

Jade rolled her eyes. "Then she needs to multitask."

Holly wished her world felt that cut and dried. "Got any ideas?" Jade did her best work under fire. Holly, not so much.

"Not me, but maybe this guy does." Jade stabbed a finger at the dream interpretation book. "You could quit letting the dreams boss you around. There's this thing called lucid dreaming, where you can plan what you want to dream about."

Holly grimaced. "I took a workshop on that once." It had been a very strange weekend full of odd rituals and chants and a lot of insomnia.

"See?" Jade grinned. "I'm not the only one with a weird background that suddenly ends up useful when you least expect it."

That was a story her best friend had managed to peddle to the Gleason powers-that-be for years. Fortunately, they never came to her office and looked in the fridge. Holly was pretty sure that trying to culture bubonic plague wasn't on the list of safe activities for corporate heiresses. "This is an insane plan."

"I make catapults out of straws. Do you know why?"

This was a much weirder Monday morning than usual, but it was somehow helping Holly find some of her absent spine. "No idea."

"It helps me think. It changes my level, gets me on the floor, makes me assess enemy territory, keeps my hands busy."

Some people took up knitting. Or bowling. "And this is a good thing?"

"We sit here in these four small walls and our brains start thinking neat, square thoughts." Jade shrugged, but her eyes were totally serious. "Straw catapults aren't square."

Or neat. Holly studied her best friend, knowing exactly how much strength and empathy and ingenuity lived in that compact, attractive package. "You're saying the answer to this isn't in the books."

"It might be. But I think it's a lot more likely that it lives in you, and if you only use the books to find it..." Jade trailed off.

Holly knew the sentence was hers to complete. "I'll find the neat, square answers." She looked at the book in Jade's hands and reached for it, sighing. She still felt queasy, but she had an ally, a direction, and maybe even the beginnings of a battle plan.

It was time to do what she did almost every Monday morning. She'd hit the books. Do some research.

And then maybe she'd go have a chat with a siren.

CHAPTER FOURTEEN

*H*olly felt utterly foolish.

Foolish, and determined, and for a researcher, utterly winging it. The dream interpretation book had been long on encouragement and short on practical details, especially if the lucid dream you wanted to have might require cooperation from outside entities who might be imaginary —or not.

She looked around her bedspread, taking in the bizarre, culturally clashing rituals she'd somehow managed to cobble together. A smudging bowl, loaded with some sticks of incense that were the closest thing to sage she could come up with on short notice. Enough candles to have cleaned out every store within walking distance. Her trio of African fertility masks, because she wanted some kick-ass women who were on her side along for the ride. A pile of mythology books with Dr. Linden's don't-believe-everything-they-tell-you author headshot on the top.

And a cup of the chamomile tea that always put her to

sleep, even on the days when dinner had involved consuming her body weight in leftover gelato, sausages, and strawberry-studded whipped cream. If nothing else, at least the tea might make a dent in her indigestion.

It was a very strange collection of armaments to take on your way to a chat with a siren, but as far as her somewhat frenzied research could tell her, if there was a protocol for such a thing, no one had ever bothered to write it down. Or they'd done it on the edge of the medieval equivalent of a shopping list and some overzealous neat freak had tossed it into history's dustbin.

Holly managed a wobbly grin—that was a good line. She should stick it in one of her papers.

Her hands shook a little as she picked up the tea. This was the kind of evening that didn't bear even passing resemblance to an academic pursuit. If she hadn't been so entirely serious about what she was trying to do, this would feel like a scene from some erstwhile amateur playwright's attempt at a cross-cultural séance.

Which was more or less what it was. It was time to figure out how to talk to the presence she felt behind the blue-gray eyes. Jade had argued briefly for trying to reach out to Mirena, but Holly figured there was no point in talking to someone who was probably at least as confused as she was. The blue-gray eyes looked like they held answers, even if a certain academic wasn't particularly sure she wanted to hear them.

For now, she was ignoring the branch of dream interpretation that thought all these characters were elements of her own psyche. Holding a séance to fetch something from your own head sounded way too much like a shortcut to multiple personality disorder.

Holly reached for the bowl and the slowly burning sticks of incense. Vanilla wafted up under her nose, and sandalwood. Earthy smells. Things that burned didn't tend to come in briny, ocean scents. Hopefully it was the thought that mattered here.

She'd done a workshop on lucid dreaming once, fascinated by the idea that dreams could be guided by waking intentions, and slightly freaked out by the directions some of her fellow workshop-goers wanted to head. They'd all been really tame compared to calling a siren ghost onto the carpet and demanding to know why she was messing with your life.

Holly sighed. She was spending way too much time worrying about the props for this particular scene. Important things first —she needed to lull herself into chamomile-induced sleep. She reached for her cup of still steaming tea and took a large sip.

If she could find her way into dreamland with intentions in her fist, perhaps the ghost she sought would come find her.

IN A THOUSAND YEARS, this had never happened.

Dedra watched, her heart beating fast and harsh under seawater-cooled skin, as the girl's face began to crystalize on the cove's white, sandy arc of beach. A face, and utterly foolish garments. Some kind of top that covered almost nothing, leaving arms and neckline bare, and decorated with small pink pigs that matched the ones on the girl's pants.

Dedra looked down at the diaphanous shawl that was all

that covered her own nakedness. At least her attire was honest, and not that of a grown woman trying to hide who she was behind the outer trappings of a small child.

She regarded the ghostly woman on the shore again. "If you wish to speak with me, I insist you put on some more appropriate clothing."

The apparition that was Holly looked down in surprise. "These are my pajamas. I didn't bring any other clothes with me."

So literal to hold so much power. "Everything here is as you think it. As you wish it." Well, not everything, but certainly enough for the girl to garb herself as she chose.

Dedra blinked as the pink pigs shimmered away and a dress appeared in their place. She wasn't up-to-date on the fashion trends of the modern world, but this looked like something one of the ladies of the big house might have worn. With a much higher neckline, and fewer frills, but similar.

Holly giggled. "Sorry. I just wanted to see if I could." The dress was replaced by a pair of tightly fitting pants and a bulky red sweater.

The old siren knew enough of what young women of this time wore on the beaches in winter not to be shocked. And they were wasting time—the girl had little experience walking in dreams, and her control would fade quickly. "You have come to me. I did not expect that."

"You should have." The girl looked up, her eyes direct and surprisingly fierce. "You've been following me around. I don't like that—it makes me feel uncomfortable."

Dedra could only do it in the most specific of circumstances, but she wasn't about to explain that to an impertinent chit. "I don't concern myself overmuch with your comfort." There were far greater things at stake here.

Holly frowned. "Are you the one sending me the strange dreams?"

That seemed safe enough to answer. "I permit you to see what once was. It is your choice whether you will see them as dreams or as something more." Dedra had long ago learned not to hope. Far too many had been willing, even eager, to dismiss what their blood knew.

Weak human hearts, preferring ease over truth.

The young woman was silent for a long while. "Mirena really existed?"

The old siren's heart caught. "She did. She is of your blood."

More silence. More eyes deep in the valley between belief and disbelief. "You know what happens. To him. To her."

It wasn't the ending the girl needed to see just yet. "What will happen to Mikel is entirely in Mirena's power." Knowledge that had universally terrified every woman touched by the curse. As much as humans railed against the gods, they rarely wanted the power to hold sway over life and death when it was given to them. "The choice will be hers."

"It's an evil choice," said Holly quietly. "Either way, she loses him."

Dedra said nothing. After a thousand years, there was nothing left to say.

"Why?" The girl's head tipped slightly to the side. "Why are you the messenger for such evil?"

She was more than that, and so much less. The only thing left standing in the way of an ancient curse's utter domination

—and its most tortured plaything. "That is my burden to bear. Yours is to choose what you will believe."

Holly's eyes narrowed. "What's that supposed to mean?"

Too much suspicion. Too much belief in her right to choose how she walked in this world. Dedra sighed. So it had been with all the women of her line in the last hundred years. This new, modern independence and a dwindling respect for powers far beyond their ken.

She had wished, far too often, that she could be one of them.

The ghostly shape on the shore started to thin, the bright red sweater and tight pants shifting back to the foolish pink pigs.

Dedra bowed her head to yet another thing she could not change. It was impressive that the girl had come at all. It remained to be seen whether that was important. Whether it would change her choices in the end.

The girl's mind was an agile one, and she believed much already—but she hadn't truly opened to what would matter most. Eventually, she would have to climb out of her mind and find the place deep inside her blood and her soul and her most primal knowing.

The place where every heart in the last thousand years had quailed.

***

SOMETIMES WHEN SHE was on stage, Holly had the odd sensation that she was two people. It had never felt more true than in this moment.

Except there seemed to be more than two of her.

There was the Holly, scared and lightheaded, who was quite convinced this was all a weird dream brought on by too many strawberries and too much time in a tight corset.

There was the Holly who desperately wanted to help a young woman escape the inexorable turning of her story's wheel.

There was the researcher, face-to-face with a real-live mythological creature.

And there was the Holly who dreaded, because she felt unfathomably sure that it wasn't only Mirena on an inexorably turning wheel.

She took a deep breath and picked the version of herself that seemed most capable of asking coherent questions. "Who are you?"

The woman with the fierce and ancient eyes took a long time to answer, and when she did, the words were tinged with sadness. "You know what I am."

"A siren."

A small shrug. "Some use that word, yes."

Researcher Holly knew some of the other words, but they didn't seem important. "How old are you?"

"A thousand of your years or so."

It wasn't the number, big though it was, that rocked Holly's core. It was what flared in blue-gray eyes as the words were said. Dedra was old and wiry and bitter and abrasive—but she was also tired.

Bone-deep exhausted.

Holly couldn't let her heart lead, not now. She had too much to learn, and she could feel herself fading. She waved a hand at Dedra's tail. "How did this happen?"

"Those who sing save the men they love. Those who sing well enough become sirens."

The academic made a horrifying leap. "Will you be the one responsible for Mikel's death if Mirena doesn't sing?"

Old eyes flashed cold fire. "That's a foolish story told by men with addled brains and manparts that have visited where they shouldn't."

Holly couldn't contain the slightly hysterical giggle. "I need to hook you up with Dr. Linden."

The siren looked utterly confused.

Not much time. "It's not important." Holly tried to focus. "What do you do, then?"

"A siren is one who has sung of her hopes and her dreams and her love, and with it, she has the power to change the life of another, to call their highest self into being." Dedra's tail undulated in the water. "In this form, that power intensifies."

Maybe the stories weren't entirely wrong. "Some of those who hear you—they die."

"Yes." The siren's face held no emotion at all. "Those who can't change, or won't, or who want our power for themselves."

Then the stories weren't entirely right, either. "Not the innocent."

"No. Never the innocent." Dedra's words snapped. "We sing with all of who we are, and we call up that flame in others. Many don't want to hear, or they fear the power they feel rising up in their own hearts, and for that, they call us evil. Dangerous. Wanton."

Holly nodded slowly. "Temptresses, calling men to their deaths. Classic patriarchal usurping of female power." Just like they'd done to the witches. If she figured out how to get out of this dream in one piece, she was going to have one heck of a paper to write. After she figured out how to cite a siren as a source.

"Your head holds much knowledge, and much wisdom." For some reason, Dedra looked sad.

Holly felt her hackles rising. "Knowledge is power."

"Not all power lives in your head." Blue-gray eyes flashed fire again. "Your song is weak. You keep your heart separate from what you know. For most of history, women have not been allowed to be all of who they are. Others have sought, always, to bind our power."

She paused and nearly hissed the last line. "You have more freedom than we've ever had—and you choose to bind yourself."

CHAPTER FIFTEEN

*H*olly stumbled into her office, not sure if she'd tripped over catapult parts, Petri dishes, or a gift from the pranksters down the hall.

It didn't much matter. This afternoon, nothing was going to get in her way.

Dedra's final words of the night before had seared themselves into Holly's mind, and had her inner academic on the rampage.

She slid the towering pile of books in her arms onto the corner of her desk. The Haversham Institute had a small library, but it had a librarian on excellent terms with all the big libraries in the vicinity and an intern who liked making road trips. One call to Evelyn this morning had produced every research tome on sirens in a hundred miles, waiting in a neat stack when Holly had finally broken loose of her round of required Tuesday morning meetings.

Normally, she enjoyed the weekly interdisciplinary free-for-alls, but on this day she had a mission, and trying to help the ancient civilizations people work out what their mysterious Viking runes might mean was not on her list.

Wrong culture. A quick Google on Vikings and sirens had pulled up nothing of interest. Probably not a surprise—if Dr. Linden was right, siren mythology took hold most fully in cultures that needed a way to compartmentalize female power. The Vikings had given their fierce women plenty of outlets.

As did the modern world, or at least this geographical part of it, even if she chose to expend that right wearing a corset and playing a whiny princess.

Holly sighed. She was taking Dedra's parting jabs too personally. Today she was going to push back from that and see what she got looking at the bigger picture. Which might well be a defense mechanism, a way not to freak out when a siren claimed you were a medieval kitchen girl's long-lost relation, but if it was a coping strategy, she could at least make it a useful one.

She tapped her fingers on her desk and contemplated the books. Last time she'd searched in all the wrong ones—the ones that would help her believe this mess wasn't true. This time she was going to try the opposite. She wasn't at all sure what she believed just yet, but she was going to try on Dedra's version as a working hypothesis.

There was a curse. Her bloodline was affected.

Every storyteller instinct she had said that her job was to find a way out. Why else would you call up an academic with an obsession for the portrayal of women in mythology?

Holly contemplated what she knew of Mirena's situation, based on what she could glean from the dream snatches she remembered. Not her usual source of research material, but she knew how much information could be hidden in the details. It was a bit like studying mythological artwork, but with moving characters.

A patriarchal society, certainly, and one where a woman's role was predetermined and largely defined by the men she ended up connected with. Fairly typical medieval society, if there was such a thing. A local center of power that ensured food, warmth, and safety for some, surrounded by a larger group of people who scrabbled pretty hard to exist.

Mythology and story took deep root in such cultures, where the struggles for life and death were daily ones and people typically felt that their destiny was largely out of their own hands.

Not that Mirena had taken the siren ultimatum any better than Holly herself would have. The kitchen girl might accept beatings from the cook with equanimity, and the social pressures of the villagers in determining the correct path of her relationship with Mikel, but she had reacted fiercely to the news that she might lose him.

Some things translated across time and culture just fine.

And it gave Holly's questing brain a place to start. Something had struck her as odd in her little dream chat with Dedra. She needed the creation stories. The legends of how sirens came to be, before Disney and the Christians had their way with things.

She knew how Dedra had come to be—but she wasn't the first. Holly's detective instincts were humming now. This wasn't the first time she'd sleuthed a story, and often what was missing told you at least as much as what was there.

Focused now, she began flipping pages, laying books out on her desk as she found passages that seemed relevant. There were ways to do the same thing online, at least with some of her sources, but that didn't spread out nearly the same way, and her brain always made its best connections by leaping from page to page.

She'd pretty much run out of desktop when she reached for the last book in her stack. Most scholars placed the first origin stories with the Assyrians. A fallen goddess, transformed by deep personal shame. Then the sirens of Greek mythology had shown up and largely shaped the narrative after that, but it seemed that the Greeks were less concerned about where sirens had come from and more focused on the danger they posed to unsuspecting sailors.

Some contradictory material on their intentions. A few hints of the Disney model, where sirens, or their more friendly mermaid personas, were sometimes helpful, or at least cute and harmless. But in most cultures, sirens took on a blend of the usual fear of female sexuality and power, mixed in with the fickle and sometimes cruel nature of the sea they lived in.

A way to explain the vicious vagaries of nature, who was usually seen as female herself, along with lots of latent and not-so-latent cultural sexism. Holly nodded—that was a theme she'd spent five fruitful years exploring, and she wasn't at all surprised to see echoes of it here.

Sexually empowered women as death, temptation, a seductive call to the dark side.

But nothing about a curse. Some dudes around Homer's time had thought sirens might die if their victims managed to hightail it out of singing range, but that didn't bear much resemblance to what she was seeing in her dreams.

Holly scrunched her nose. Enough of the mythology had

sirens associating with gods and goddesses that it wasn't hard to imagine a curse had landed somewhere—the Greek deities had been wildly fond of hurling doozies at each other, and often perfectly innocent bystanders got thoroughly cursed in the crossfire. But if such a thing had happened to create the sirens, no one had bothered to write it down.

It wasn't an unusual problem when you were trying to track the feminine through history. The details that mattered, the ones that got recorded, were the ones that related to the wider, often very male-focused culture. How some poor siren ended up singing on a rock was far less relevant than what danger she might pose to some random guy in her vicinity.

Which was also interesting, because in Holly's dreams, Mikel wasn't the sirens' focus. Mirena was. And her song was supposed to bring life to her love, not death.

Clues in what wasn't said.

Holly ran her fingers down pages, reading quickly again. Looking for evidence that the sirens had ever targeted their own sex, or for that matter, that they targeted anyone at all. Dedra's eyes were old and bitter and had seen far too much, but something in Holly deeply resisted casting the old siren as the villain here. The messenger, yes, or maybe someone stuck between a rock and a hard place and forced to put others there with her. The story behind the easy story everyone told. Or possibly, the story women told each other when no one else was listening.

Holly paused, wondering if she was just headed down an academic rabbit hole, or something more valuable than that.

Maybe she wasn't supposed to figure out how to help Mirena escape the curse. Maybe she was just supposed to get the story right. Holly's fingers tapped pages. She'd need far more than what she had here to do that, but it wouldn't be the first time she'd followed an idle line or two of some lone researcher's speculation—or her own.

She leaned back, sighing. That felt important, but it didn't feel right. Something was driving her, and her usual answer when that happened was to follow the words, dig into the data—but that was when the intended ending was a neatly notated academic paper.

That just wasn't what she was supposed to be doing here. Some of what she was thinking smelled right. There was a curse that needed to be broken, a way out found for Mirena and her farmer love so they could live happily ever after.

But Holly had to believe that Dedra's parting words mattered. This story was calling Holly *out* of her head, not into it.

Carefully, she closed and restacked her books, and then laid her hand down on the volume of Dr. Linden's sassy academic snark. Parts of the answer might be here, but somehow this wasn't right, and she couldn't even blame that niggling sureness on lurking blue-gray eyes.

This time, it was pure Holly Castas gut instincts doing the talking.

CHAPTER SIXTEEN

*H*olly slid in the back door of the Inkspot, her eyes already on the lookout for Monster. His truck had been in the parking lot, and it was pretty typical for him to arrive early, checking and rechecking prop lists, scenery repairs, and whatever other esoteric things he did to keep their backstage efforts running smoothly.

The interior was dark and quiet, with only basic lights pointed at the stage. She made her way through the seats and breathed in the slightly stale odor of a theater patiently waiting for an audience. It was a smell she loved, no matter how it might wrinkle the noses of those less inclined to hang out in old concrete buildings.

She'd always imagined this one with the personality of a Victorian coquette underneath all the drab. A temptress, just waiting for someone to recognize what lay beneath the surface.

Kind of like what Dedra had said, only in reverse.

Holly's shoulders squirmed up toward her ears. She liked

the compartments of her life. She had layers, just like the Inkspot. Blending them together meant too many things spilling out of boxes they didn't quite fit into. The discontent of an academic forced to break stories down into their component parts, denying the mystery of the whole. The friction of a community theater lifer who gritted her teeth at some of the stories they wasted their talent on.

Nobody would thank her for being a princess rebel, for rewriting the parts so they better fit her soul.

Holly sighed. She'd wanted to do it often enough. And while most of her fellow cast members might not care overmuch, she knew they wouldn't protest, either. Amateur playwrights were just as welcome as amateur actors. It was her own desire to fit, to be the round peg destined comfortably for the round hole, that was the problem.

Dedra didn't see that part. The old siren had only seen the compromises of Holly's life, the corners quietly sandpapered to fit. She hadn't seen the why, the deep desire to truly belong to a community that knew who she was and how she worked and appreciated her for it.

The words of the siren taunted her.

Annoyed, Holly hummed a low note under her breath. It reverberated weirdly in the nearly empty theater, picking up strange harmonic echoes.

She rolled her eyes. The Inkspot was far too mundane to be haunted.

She let a whole line loose this time, picking up a riff from nowhere in particular and dancing it into the dark corners on purpose. If there were ghosts, she might as well make sure they could hear her. Her voice might lack talent, but she'd never had a problem with volume.

More strange harmonics, and an itch traveling under her skin as her random melody picked up steam. She remembered the tales of the *lillevenn*, small Norse creatures who sang the Northern Lights into being.

Song was energy, just like story.

She could feel the crackling energy of this impromptu song building now, pulling out notes she'd had no idea lived inside her, ones that traveled up into the high reaches, enough to pierce through the workmanlike concrete ceilings and find the stars, and others deep enough to make the foundations tremble.

This was not a song with the nice, polite ranges of your average theater musical.

She stepped into the center stage spotlight, feeling the inexorable need for this moment to be fully seen.

And let loose with all that was building under her skin. A rainforest jungle of sound, drumbeat and pounding rain and the almost silent sounds of decay and birth, leaves unfurling in the damp dark and victors reaching for the sun. A pungent, howling cacophony of sound that could not possibly be Holly Castas—and yet was.

It came to an abrupt halt after a sliding run that left Holly breathless, resonant, and staggered by what had just happened. Every hair on her body, even the tiny ones on her upper lip, vibrated in the energy of what she'd just created.

A furtive sound, promptly squelched, came out of the silence behind her.

Holly spun around, seeking the source, and found Monster's head popped up over the back of the director's chair, his mouth gaping.

She tried not to squirm—her body was shaking badly enough as it was.

"Wow." Monster seemed to be struggling to find more words. "You can sing. Like *really* sing. I've never heard anything like that before."

And he never would again. "Just something I was trying out. The acoustics are good in here." Even as she said it, she could feel the newly bold pieces of her soul protesting. She was sandpapering again. Taking off the sharp edges.

Denying some important part of who she was.

Monster just watched her cautiously and said nothing.

Holly did the only thing she could do with the mess that was the song's aftermath—she turned regally and exited stage right. She'd go find a corner to hole up in, well out of Monster's way, and stuff herself back into the skin of a flighty, hopelessly naive, overly whiny princess. Because real life didn't come with an infinity of roles to choose from, and being that princess helped her be a reasonably fulfilled, happy human being.

It was good to step into the skin of Holly as she might be if the world had no limits, no rules, no realities. But it was also good to help that Holly find her place in the real world.

If that dulled the shine of her song a bit, that was okay. The woman who'd called her on the sandpapering had a point, and Holly knew she'd need to let that settle a little, work its way into all the cracks and crevices where she processed things that mattered. But Dedra was also a tired, washed-up, very bitter figment of most people's imaginations. Being all of who you were, singing that into being, obviously had some pretty treacherous downsides.

Holly felt the tremors easing. She shouldn't have to apologize for taking some care with her life. That was what made her different from cats, toddlers, and divas. A little more tempestuousness in her life might be a good thing, but she didn't want to live there permanently. The world could only contain so many divas, and Holly Castas had never wanted to be one of them.

She breathed out, calmer now, and headed for the makeshift change rooms backstage. First to figure out if some duct tape could give her a little more breathing room in her corset, and then she'd see if Monster needed help gluing things or shuffling them around before the rest of the crew arrived for final rehearsal.

She wound around the dark piles of cables and discarded props without disturbing anything. As chaotic as it might look, she knew there was a system back here, and stagehands who would growl in absentia if she touched anything.

Steady steps back into her regular-person life.

"TOUCH THE TREE AND DIE."

Holly jumped back from the tree limb she'd been about to use to support herself as she fixed a lump in her stocking. Not a fashion issue she normally dealt with, but high-heeled boots and baggy wool stockings were not a fun mix, especially when it required several curse words and a minor act of God to bend over in her corset. She looked over at stage left, where the admonishment had come from. "Good vocal delivery, but you need more emotion to make it really convincing."

"Everyone's a critic." Jamie stepped out of the shadows, grinning. "I just spent an hour gluing on all the branches Ian lopped off in the last week. I make no promises that they'll stay on if you do anything more than breathe on them."

She hopped over to use his shoulder for balance while she adjusted her stocking instead. "Don't you believe in crazy glue? I'm pretty sure we buy it by the pound."

He shifted his feet apart to be a more stable leaning post. "Monster keeps that under lock and key, and he seems to have disappeared. At this point, the tree is mostly held together with chewing gum and duct tape."

Holly was a firm believer in the powers of duct tape, but she also knew better than to mess with the prop guys. "I'll try to encourage Ian to accidentally lop off something else instead."

"Please don't." He looked down at her legs, fetchingly clad in hand-knit wool that could only very charitably be called stockings. "I like your limbs quite a bit, and I'd hate to see one of them chopped off."

Guys didn't flirt with Holly every day, especially when she was hopping around in a princess costume and some grandmother's purloined woolies. She managed to get both feet back on the ground and hoped he thought her pink cheeks were from sock exertion. "Thanks, I think."

He looked at her, eyes running slowly over her face in a way that didn't do anything to calm down the color in her cheeks. "So, what's it like, playing a character who's so different from who you really are?"

That was an interesting and oddly loaded question, especially when she was still trying to work her way through Dedra's parting blast. "Even when I was a little kid, I loved sliding myself into a story, and acting gives me a chance to do that as a grownup. I get to step out of my own skin and be whoever I want to be." That was her pat answer, but tonight, it felt incomplete.

Jamie's head tilted curiously, as if he waited for the words she hadn't yet said.

Holly huffed out a breath, blowing her curls off her face. "I guess, in the end, Julietta's not really that much different from me. She's whinier, and younger, and the outer trappings are different." She fingered the skirt of her gown.

His eyes hadn't moved from her face.

She gulped and kept going. "But what Julietta really wants is to be seen and loved for exactly who she is. To be special in the world, and to have someone notice and for her life to have meaning. If I can show the audience that, how she's the same inside as each of us are..." She trailed off, not sure how to finish. "That's why I do this, I think. To show how we're really all the same."

His head tipped an inch to the left, and nothing more.

She suddenly felt foolish, standing there in a too-tight corset and droopy woolen tights, talking about her still-forming philosophy of life. "Sorry. Sometimes I go all wordy and deep when someone was just looking for a quick answer."

He smiled slowly. "Not this someone."

Holly swallowed the need to make more excuses for words she had truly meant. "Thanks."

He shrugged. "I grow spinach for a living. I like to think that makes a difference in the world too."

The energy between them coalesced into something she could almost touch.

Somewhere in the background, Monster put out the call for his stage guys.

Holly wiggled from one high-heeled boot to the other,

feeling something quite different than foolish, but no less antsy. "You probably need to go." She could hear the activity in the wings getting more dramatic. "I'll see if I can keep Ian from mauling your tree."

Jamie's smile was amused, low voltage, and it did something very interesting to the lands inside her corset. "Don't try too hard. The world needs as many courageous, bumbling knights as it can get."

She closed her eyes as she walked away, hugging his words close to her heart. Somehow when Jamie saw Ian and Holly on the stage, he saw the greater thing they were trying to hint at. The universal story they were trying to tell, the greater truths that defined what made human hearts human.

The ways in which she was Julietta. And Mirena. And Dedra. And they were her.

She wasn't sure why that particular insight mattered, but it did—and it wasn't just Holly Castas who thought so. For the first time, the pendant around her neck felt warm. Comfortable.

Like maybe it belonged there.

CHAPTER SEVENTEEN

*M*irena stepped through the kitchen door that led to the back courtyard, an enormous basket of laundry in her hands and gladness in her heart. At this time of year, any small errand that got her outside was pure pleasure, even when the morning sun's rays were weak yet. She'd drop the laundry off in the wagon headed to the village and take the path around through the front gardens on her return.

A small bit of laziness that no one was likely to notice on this morning. The house staff were airing all the linens and rugs and tapestries for fall, and even Cook was mostly smart enough to stay out of their way. They'd set up a buffet of cold foods in the main hall, enough to feed villagers and house staff both. On this day, every set of hands was needed as they got the big house cleaned and settled and ready for the coming days of autumn.

Mirena didn't mind, not when the crispness hadn't hit the morning air yet. That would come, and with it, the aching in her legs would increase, but for now, she could do her work and pretend that summer was an endless, beautiful thing.

Perhaps by next summer's turn, she'd be beating the rugs and bedcovers of her new home. Not that they'd likely own a rug for many years yet, but she could always hope. Stepping onto the cold floor of a morning was one of the things her legs most disliked. Other women yearned for fancy stitching or a bit of beautiful fabric or a sturdy new pot, but her desires would always run to warmth and comfort.

They'd be fine, even without a rug. Mikel would chop all the wood necessary for a steady winter fire, and she knew all the tricks to getting the most warmth from the smallest amount of wood. And her friend Bethany made sturdy felted slippers, and was always willing to trade for some of Mirena's baking.

It would take a lot of baking to cover a pair of slippers for Mikel. Perhaps that was a trade she could arrange soon. It wasn't strictly permitted, given that they weren't handfasted yet, but everyone knew that was just a matter of time, and slippers were a practical necessity, not his hand sliding improperly up the warm skin of her legs.

Although heavens knew there were days that felt like necessity too.

All this waiting. Mirena tipped her head up to the sun. Perhaps it was better that the warm days turned the corner to chill. She'd be that much closer to having her man to keep her warm at night.

It took a moment for the pounding footsteps to register.

She turned as Brenin, best friend of Mikel's youngest brother, flew to her side. He paused, poised like a hawk on his bare toes, ready to take off again, and gasped for breath. "Mirena, come quick. Tirenne says you have to come."

Mirena's heart congealed into cold dread. Tirenne was the village's best healer. She never sent for anyone this urgently unless the news was very bad. She dropped her laundry basket, heedless of dumping linens all over the ground, and clutched Brenin's shoulders. "Who is it—who's hurt?"

His eyes were big and brown and wide in a horribly white face. "Mikel. There was a rock slide at the cliffs. He got hit in the head."

She hadn't even known he would be at the cliffs today. She let go of Brenin and fled down the narrow path. He yelled something at her back, but she didn't pause long enough to hear it. Her feet moved toward the village as fast as a young boy's, ignoring the pain shooting up her legs as they protested such abuse.

She knew they wouldn't fail her now. Mikel needed her.

All her senses receded as she ran. She heard nothing, saw nothing, felt nothing. Only speed. Only the knowing that her man was hurt and the healer had called for her.

Her feet took her, straight and true, into the doorway of the healer's hut. The dark dim and the line of broad backs stopped her run—and then the smell hit, the indefinable, unmistakable odor of a body on the edge of death. People said you couldn't smell death, but they were wrong. Mirena's nose had woken up with nightmares for months after her mother passed, the horror of that smell permeating every breath she took in the dark.

Only sunlight chased it away. Tirenne's hut was dark. Too dark.

Mirena elbowed her way between the broad backs, heedless of who she might be pushing out of the way. A few harsh, surprised mutters, and then the men of the village recognized her and gave way.

The sight of Mikel on the healer's narrow cot nearly felled her where she stood.

He looked so pale, and so still, and so very, very small.

She felt arms reaching out. Kind ones, gentle ones, leading her to a small stool at his left side. Mikel's mother already sat on his right, two of his sisters fisting handfuls of their skirts as they gazed, frantic, on the rock that had always been their older brother.

Or rather, what was left of him after the rocks fell.

She could see the cuts and scratches, the deep gouges where his bare skin had fought with falling debris and lost. But it was his stillness that scared her down to the bones. She looked over at Tirenne's bent form, stirring something on the hearth.

The old healer met her gaze, eyes grim. "We'll know more if he wakes up. It's good that you're here."

Calm words, and simple ones, but still, Mikel's sisters breathed out in raspy panic.

Mirena could not find it in herself to breathe.

Her eyes slid back to the still, white face, and to the big hands laid out on the blanket at his sides. "Is it all right if I touch him?"

"Don't be foolish." The healer's words were brusque, but the hand on Mirena's shoulder was kind. "No one has ever died from a touch, at least not while they were in my care."

Gingerly, Mirena slid her fingers under his—and fought off the need to vent the contents of her stomach all over Tirenne's floor at the cold limpness. It was the hand of a dead man, not her strong and handsome farmer. "He's cold." Her throat rattled as she spoke.

"It's good for him to stay cool." Tirenne adjusted the pillow under his head. "The fever will come soon enough, and then we'll have a job to do to keep him comfortable."

She'd helped nurse enough sick villagers to know what that would take. "I need to stay." Cook would have fits.

"It will be done." The old healer sounded very certain, which tightened the cold dread in Mirena's heart even more.

Tirenne thought Mikel was going to die.

CHAPTER EIGHTEEN

*S*he felt like a complete idiot. And she wished Monster didn't drive like a really law-abiding grandmother. Holly glanced over at the quiet man behind the wheel of his big truck and grimaced. "Sorry to drag you away from whatever you planned on doing today."

He shrugged and looked amused. "It was either that or spend an hour on the phone calming you down."

She grimaced. The early morning text she'd sent him might have been a little bit frantic—the consequences of waking up with wet cheeks and the horrified sense that the stakes had just catapulted themselves into the stratosphere. "Sorry. I had a bad dream, and I wasn't thinking very clearly when I woke up."

"So you said." He looked as calm as he always did. Even opening nights with a dozen crazy community theater actors never shook him. "Are you going to apologize all the way to Jamie's place, or can we talk about something else now?"

She felt her face slide into a grin. "If you dislike drama so much, how did they manage to rope you into working at the Inkspot?"

He shrugged again. "The pay's good."

He got paid just as much as the rest of them. Holly leaned back against the old, well-worn leather bench seat, pretty sure there was a story in this she hadn't heard yet—and maybe if she went chasing it, her mind would have something different to do than running Mikel's still, white face on repeat. "So you spend hundreds of hours every year making sure we have the best-managed backstage in all of New England for a couple of Matteo's Christmas cookies?" They were really good cookies, but still.

Monster's cheeks turned faintly pink. "No big deal. And I get more than two cookies."

Holly snickered. "Clearly, I need to renegotiate my contract."

He glanced her way for the first time. "You should. You're really good."

She raised a surprised eyebrow, and because she wasn't a total idiot, took a sniff of the vibe in the truck. Monster was a very cool guy, but she'd never read any hint of interested from him.

"That was an actual comment on your talent," he said wryly. "Occasionally, we people of the male persuasion manage to say something nice even when we don't want in your pants."

She knew she was staring, but there wasn't much she could do about it. Guys who ground sausage and moved scenery around didn't tend to be all that psychic. "Thanks. I think."

This time, he full-on laughed. "It works out well. I have my eye on someone else, and I'm pretty sure we're driving out to see the guy who's caught your interest."

If it was a distraction she wanted, one had just landed with both feet. Holly could feel the wheels of her brain churning, trying to solve the mystery that had just been conveniently dumped in her lap. Monster spent all his time at the Inkspot, just like the rest of them, but if there had been a hint of theater romance in the air, Marion or Zed or Abby would have sniffed it out long ago. "It can't be one of the actors."

He just grinned and kept staring down the road.

"Come on. Dish."

He cocked an eyebrow. "Really? You woke me up at the crack of dawn on my day off, you're playing hooky from work to come pick cherry tomatoes, and it's *my* love life you think we should talk about?"

Absolutely. The alternatives totally didn't bear mentioning. "Kinda, yeah."

He snorted. "Whatever."

Jade would have duct-taped her to a chair and made her spill. "I don't think I've ever heard you talk this much."

"Hard to get a word in edgewise most places."

She could only imagine, especially if you weren't comfortable yelling over half a dozen other voices. Or maybe he didn't need to hear the sound of his own thoughts, spoken out loud, to be happy.

She smiled. Whatever his reasons were, she was glad he'd climbed out of his shell today. He'd been nothing but calm, generous, and understanding on a morning when she'd felt really rattled, and in doing so, had managed to land her back on something resembling solid ground. Which was a pretty good trick while meandering down the road in an old, dirty truck.

The sausage guy had unplumbed depths—or at least really under-appreciated ones.

It was going to be an interesting day.

JAMIE LOOKED SURPRISED when they clambered out of Monster's truck, but happy enough to see them. He also looked like he'd been up for hours.

Holly tried to figure out how to explain her sudden appearance—and her deep, pernicious relief that he was upright and walking.

Monster grabbed a stack of pint baskets out of the box in the back of his truck. "I'll go pick cherry tomatoes and stay out of your hair."

Jamie blinked. "Okay." He watched the back of his friend as he wandered off, presumably in the direction of the tomato patch, and then raised an eyebrow at Holly.

Maybe when the really weird hit the fan, truth was the best policy. "I had a strange dream. Some guy with your face got really badly hurt, so I wanted to see if you were okay. I didn't know how to reach you, so I called Monster, and he said he was coming out this way so I could catch a ride and see for myself." She stopped—somewhere in there, sharing of truth had turned into babbling.

He looked at her for a minute, and then one corner of his mouth quirked up into a grin. "My mom warned me about you flaky actress types."

It wasn't the words that warmed her, it was the tone—

accepting and welcoming and full of gentle good humor. Inviting her to laugh at herself, and to rest easy.

Apparently, the man did flaky actress just fine. "Sorry, I know it's kind of a loopy story."

He shrugged. "It brought you to my farm, so I'll take it."

There was invitation there—and something that felt far too much like Mikel at the handfasting dance. Earthy and open. Steadiness and sunshine. Which was weird, but it beat imagining him unconscious on a straw pallet with gashes everywhere she looked. Holly scrunched up her eyes, trying to kick the rest of her dream ghosts to the curb. "You look like you're busy doing stuff this morning—can I help?" It was a glorious day, and if she was playing hooky, she might as well do it right.

"Sure." Jamie nodded at a small trail that ran off the drive-way. "Want to pick green beans? That was the next thing on my list, or the next fun one, anyhow."

She was a little afraid to ask. "What does that mean you're skipping?"

He chuckled as he fell into step behind her. "Trying to exert some discipline in the blackberry patch, and finding my missing rooster."

She knew enough about blackberries to stay far away from trying to wrangle their prickly, grow-anywhere bushes. "Can't you just wave a sexy chicken at your rooster's last known location or something?" She turned around as she walked, grinning at him. "That could totally be fun."

His lips quirked. "I'm pretty sure my girls are pissed off at him, and that's why he's nowhere to be found."

Ah. "That whole hen-pecked thing is literal, is it?"

He grinned. "Green beans or chickens?"

Far be it from her to get in the way of poultry relations. "Green beans sound like less drama." Today, that seemed like a good thing.

He moved up beside her as the pathway widened. Holly's eyes wandered, getting more curious as they walked past a stretch of wildflowers and a small grassy meadow and approached what looked like very organized, well-tended fields. A farm, rather than a garden, although on a much smaller scale than she'd seen on road trips through the Midwest to visit her cousins.

Jamie took a short offshoot off the path and approached the door of a decent-sized tool shed. She stepped inside, enjoying the shadowed, earthy atmosphere that was a nice antidote to the cold and threatening mists of her dreams.

A different kind of energy lived here. A different kind of power. "No tractors?"

"Nope. Organic farming at the scale I do it is done mostly by hand." He reached for a thing that she was pretty sure was a hoe. "I have a family who helps me out most of the year, but they're off visiting relatives in Mexico this month."

Holly's agile brain offered up all the newspaper articles she'd read on migrant workers and their appalling treatment.

"I try to do it right," he said quietly, glancing her way. "They live in a comfortable cottage right beside mine, I pay Miguel and Paula wages and a share of the farm's profits, and all three of their kids are in school and doing really well. They've worked with me for six years now."

She felt like the questionable stuff on the bottom of someone's boot. "It sounds like you've worked really hard to build something that can support all of you." She'd seen evidence of his local marketing efforts and tasted enough of his produce to know he was creating a good thing. "I apologize profusely for my stupid assumptions."

"Part of being an organic farmer is believing that I can make a difference by what I do with my hands every day." He shrugged. "Treating the people I work with like fellow human beings seems like part of that. Plenty don't, and I know that too."

She smiled. "Hearing that, loud and clear." The energy of this place, its story, didn't come from just the land.

He handed her a small tool that looked like a shrunken shovel, and a big wicker basket. "The basket's for collecting the green beans. The trowel is for displacing any resident slugs you see."

Oh, boy. "Time to prove I'm not a flaky actress?"

"Something like that." He grinned and led the way to thriving rows of green beans not far from the shed.

Holly leaned over and snapped a couple off, keeping a watchful eye out for slugs. She crunched down on one of the beans, enjoying its wet, crunchy goodness. "Anything special I need to know?"

He raised an eyebrow. "You eat raw green beans?"

When they were this good, absolutely. "Easier than cooking them."

He grinned and reached for the other one in her hand. "A woman after my own heart."

She made a mostly fake swipe at retrieving it. "Hey, buster —pick your own snack."

He was still laughing when he reached down and started picking plump, dew-wet beans at a speed that made her realize she'd better get moving if she wanted to be anything more than pretty decoration.

They worked together in a silence that felt companionable, the warm sun slowly heating up her shoulders and drying the dew off the green beans. The basket at her feet filled appreciably. It was satisfying in a way that watching word count go up as she wrote a paper just wasn't. Tangible. Something that fed an atavistic desire to hunt, gather, provide. The simple pleasures of getting her hands dirty.

Holly looked at her thumbs and forefingers, streaked in dirt and light green juice, and grinned. Matteo would have fits if that didn't wash off. Totally out of character for a whiny princess.

She looked over at Jamie, who had finished his row of green beans long ago and moved on to tending a small plot of summer spinach grown in the shade of the shed.

She watched his hands, competently doing whatever it was they did to make baby spinach leaves happy, and felt the edges of dream catch her again. It was all too easy to imagine another man, hundreds of years ago, doing exactly the same thing.

Holly pushed back against the encroaching images that felt far too much like memory. Jamie was not Mikel. This was no different than when a paper or an acting role tried to get temperamental or out of control. She was in charge of deciding what she let her mind and heart tangle with.

Heat rose up behind that thought. She got to choose.

Jamie was not Mikel, she wasn't a kitchen girl in rough-woven linen and bare feet, and this needed to stop. Before she went crazy, and before whatever the heck was going on here pulled her any deeper into its web.

She would deal with that, but first, she would pick another row of green beans and soak up a day of dirt and sunshine and let the strength that lived here soothe her soul. Jamie's farm was pretty much the antithesis of salty ocean waters and the threat that lived there.

There were all kinds of power, and this time, Holly Castas was collecting hers.

HOLLY STRODE onto the small bridge that spanned the river and stopped, feeling a bit like Batman, or Heathcliff from *Wuthering Heights*. The wind was cooperating, whipping her light jacket around her legs and streaming her hair out into the night fog.

She didn't feel foolish this time.

Monster had dropped her off at the curb and managed not to ask any of the dozen or so questions she could practically hear cranking the gears in his mind.

She'd gotten out, leaving him and his treasure trove of cherry tomatoes in silence. She didn't know any of the answers. She just knew that this was the closest thing to sea water running in her little town, and she was doing this next part on her turf. She'd spent a really nice day with a good and interesting man, and be damned if she wanted to see his face in her dreams tonight.

Especially lying on a bed looking like he was at death's door.

This needed to stop. She would help Mirena and Dedra however she could, but there were lines.

She closed her eyes and brought up the siren's face in as much detail as she could. Sharp cheekbones shaping skin the color of desert sand, tangled brown hair accustomed to using sea gales as a comb, and the piercing gaze of blue-gray eyes that knew how to see everything.

"I need to talk to you." Holly only felt a little nuts talking to an empty river. She'd brought Dedra to her once, and this time she wasn't in the mood for chamomile tea and pretty candles and lying down on her bed. If her life was coming apart at some very weird seams, she at least wanted a chance to play her lines on her feet.

She focused in again on her mental image of Dedra's face. "You know things I need to know, and I'm done with you being all cryptic and only sending me what you want me to see." Holly wasn't at all sure when she'd come to the conclusion that the siren was controlling the flow of the dreams, but it fit the story in a way that she wasn't going to question—at least not while she was trying to summon a thousand-year-old woman with a tail.

She laid her hands on the railing and tugged on ancient eyes and the presence behind them.

For an elongated, hazed moment, something on the other end of the line tugged back.

And then it was gone, and she was just a woman in a windbreaker standing on a bridge looking down at a little stretch of urban river.

Holly let out a long, slow breath and then a string of curses that would have offended people in at least four different eras.

This wasn't the story she wanted to be cast in.

This needed to stop.

CHAPTER NINETEEN

*T*he girl understood so much—and so very, very little.

Dedra shook with the force of Holly's call and her deep need to resist it. It would not do to let the girl think her power could help her escape this.

The touch of the curse was absolute. Resistance was dangerous, and it was futile. Many had tried, and no one had ever won. The wheel turned without mercy, and an old siren had been its pawn for every turn.

She could not hold out much longer, and if she failed—if she could not produce another to take her place—every line of every siren ever born would be forever hunted by a curse no longer fettered, and no one would even know why. She had taken the burden from each of her sisters as they let go, unable to find one of their line to keep singing. Stood for all those who would come from their blood, even as she shuddered under the weight of it.

Surrounded by their skulls, she sang of her fury and theirs, her anguish, her pummeling need, hurling it all into the uncaring wind for years beyond imagining.

She had so little left.

So much rode on the choices of a girl named after an insignificant red berry.

Dedra quivered as echoes of Holly's last angry call careened off the waves and got swallowed.

And wondered.

So much about this particular time was strange. Different. Holly didn't yet love, and she fought with her brain, not her heart. But she could hear the dreams, and that only ever happened when the curse had chosen.

Always, it picked the brightest and the best. The foolish girl stood on the edge of a filthy, polluted little river, and still she yanked with a power that had Dedra shaking as she held tight to her ocean waters. She wanted to go, to sit in that silly stream and shake the daughter of her blood into belief.

They never believed in time.

Most never even heard. Holly was the first in a hundred years. And of the few who made it this far, most quit with what came next.

Dedra felt the shudder rising up in her chest, the frantic, desperate beating of a truth that she no longer had the strength to hide.

She couldn't wait a hundred years more for the next one.

The girl knew more than most. Her brightness, her drive, were pushing things fast, so much faster than usual. Holly had a strength of conviction capable of demanding that the world listen and a fortitude that had a thousand-year-old siren shaking in her boots.

Dedra no longer dared to hope those things would matter.

In the end, the curse would strangle them both.

CHAPTER TWENTY

*M*ikel's mother walked slowly out of the healer's hut into the first rays of dawn, leaning heavily on her youngest daughter. Mirena watched them go from her perch on a stool at Tirenne's hearth. She had stirred the pot the whole night through. The old healer had sent some kind of word to Cook—one that had been returned with two loaves of fresh bread and the message that Mirena might stay as long as she was needed.

The kindness had nearly finished what Mikel's still, wan face had started.

"Steady up, girl—you're not the first to have your man lying on my healing bed, and you won't be the last." Tirenne had also been up all night, but she looked entirely unaffected by the creeping exhaustion that had seeped into everyone else's bones in the dark. "He'll do better without his mother and sister whimpering over him, and I suspect you might as well."

Mirena had been whimpering too, just more quietly. She had more practice hiding her grief. "They're afraid."

"Of course they are." Tirenne lifted a ladle full of broth from the pot over the fire. "This will bring strength back to him when he wakes."

If he woke. Mirena knew well that the broth was something a girl of five or six summers could have tended. The healer's kindness terrified her. "Is there anything more I can do?"

"Aye." A pause as Tirenne collected some clean rags and lifted the lid off a small kettle that had been steeping half the night. "You can move closer to the bed and hold his hand while I change the dressings on the worst of his gashes. He's got a hard head, your man does, but if he wants to keep his leg, we need to draw out what will try to settle there."

Mirena's throat choked nearly closed. She hadn't known the gashes tucked away under the covers were that serious. Mikel was a farmer—to lose a leg was almost a fate worse than death.

Tirenne poured hot tea over the rags, now in a shallow bowl, and set the kettle back down on the rough stone counter she used to assemble most of her remedies. "You're strong enough to hear the truth. And strong enough to keep it out of your eyes when your man wakes up."

If he woke. Mirena swallowed. She could do this for Mikel. Ignoring the cramping, she crawled down from the stool and limped over to the edge of the bed, looking around for somewhere to sit that her legs could manage after the long, hard night.

"The bed is big enough for two." Something different colored Tirenne's voice now. "You'll be in his soon enough, and no one will think it improper while he's weaker than a baby and drinking gruel."

Those people didn't know Mikel very well—he was always reaching out to touch her, even when his arms could barely move after a full day bringing in the harvest. Innocent touches, by the standards of the villagers, but she knew what he wanted. The thought brought a smile to Mirena's face, and resolve to her heart. With more steadiness than she'd felt all night, she sat down at his side and took his limp fingers into hers. They were warmer now, and soon enough, they would be reaching for her again.

She was done with imagining anything else. Done with fearing that she might have caused anything else.

She heard the quiet harrumph of Tirenne's approval, and then the healer peeled back one side of the blanket. Mirena blanched when she saw what lay under the bandages. There was a reason the healer had kept those hidden.

Tirenne's competent hands laid the tea-dipped cloth down on the worst of Mikel's wounds. Her fingers deftly squeezed out more hot tea over the cloth even as the man on the bed moaned. The sound drove deep into Mirena's heart. So much pain.

The healer's hands didn't pause in their work. "This will help draw out the festering so it can mend cleanly."

When wounds didn't mend cleanly, men often died. Mirena clutched Mikel's hand more tightly. Surely fingers that knew how to be so warm, so strong, could not be hovering on death's door.

The fear she'd chased away all the long night flooded her belly again. Her free hand crept to the pendant around her throat.

The healer's eyes followed the movement—and something dark and worried entered her gaze. "Your mama wore one such as that once."

Dread curled in Mirena's belly. "That's not possible."

A long silence. "When you're as old as I am, you begin to believe that there are very few things in this life that are not possible. Hers was a different color, but made by the same hand." Tirenne's fingers squeezed more tea onto the poultice on Mikel's leg. "And when she wore it, she carried the same look in her eyes as yours have now. Guilt, and a terrible sadness. I always thought it was her worrying for the babe on the way." Her eyes fell to Mirena's belly.

Realization landed, and denial, hot and fierce. "We're not handfasted yet. We've done nothing improper."

"That's a shame." Tirenne chuckled quietly. "Your man on the bed there seems like he might know enough of what he's about so that you'd enjoy it."

Never in her life had Mirena heard such blunt words. "I wouldn't know," she answered stiffly.

"Your mother did." The healer laid a thick piece of wool cloth over the tea poultice, satisfied with her work for now. "And don't you be judging her for it. Not all men have the patience of this one, and not all the lasses either, and you're here on this earth because of it. She loved your father well enough."

Mirena had so many questions, and all of them bubbled up and tried to force themselves out her throat at once. She picked the most important one. "You knew my father?" It had been the one subject on which the village had always been entirely silent, at least where a young girl's ears could hear.

"Aye. A soldier passing through for the summer caught her

eye." Tirenne turned abruptly to stir the pot over her fire. "He's dead and gone many years now. Lost to a brigand's sword months before you were born." A long pause that held only the bubbling sounds and smells of the healer's gruel. "Your mama loved him very much. Her grief was wild when he passed, and I thought she might lose you, but even then you were a stubborn little thing. You stuck, all through the nights when your mother clutched that pendant of hers and fought with the fevers and the sorrow that tried to take her."

Tirenne was watching her now, like one of the hawks that flew high in the hills waiting for its prey to move, only gentler. "She was never quite the same again after he died. I always believed that she grieved him still."

Mirena had seen that sadness in her mother's eyes and never known what put it there, but having one of the great mysteries of her young life explained passed by almost unnoticed. Her mind could only make room for two terrible, drumming thoughts.

Mama had chosen life. And the man she loved had died.

It had not been sadness riding in her eyes, or not only that —there Tirenne was wrong. It had been guilt. Mama had been given the same awful choice. Mirena's mind could barely hold the thinking of it. Her fingers spasmed, one hand linked with Mikel's and the other clutched around the pendant at her throat.

Mama had chosen life. And the man she loved had died.

CHAPTER TWENTY-ONE

*F*rom the depths of sleep, Holly yanked. She didn't know what she yanked on, exactly, but she wasn't letting the story go. Not this time.

The dream that was not a dream shimmered, shifting.

She yanked again. She was not waking up. There was more than one way to find out what came next, and she wasn't leaving until she'd seen it.

The mists started to shift.

Holly followed them and found herself on Mirena's beach. Or rather, the beach was behind her. She was perched on the rocks farther out, the ones no longer protected by cliff and cove. She gulped as waves crashed hard against her perch.

"You will not fall in." Dedra sounded amused, pitching her voice to be heard over the turbulent waters. "And if you do, I presume your blood still remembers how to swim."

It did. In a nice, safe, waveless swimming pool. Holly wished for bare feet, the better to hold her to the rocks—and then, in the way of dreams, she had them. The pink pig pajamas, she left alone. This visit wasn't about her sense of fashion, and the pigs were cozy—a reminder of a part of who she was that Dedra didn't seem to understand or respect.

She looked at the siren and let some of that flash in her eyes. "What happens to Mikel?"

A shrug, from shoulders still wet with sea water. "That is not mine to tell."

That was ridiculous. "You're the one pushing me this story —surely you know how it ends."

Silence, buttressed by the steely resolve of a thousand years.

Holly felt her feet sinking into the rocks, trying to find purchase in this place of crashing waters and briny damp and power that wasn't her own. She was an alien here, a stranger in a strange land.

She fought for her inner warrior, or her inner flaky princess, or any version of Holly Castas that knew how to walk in the irrational and be strong.

And shook her head, bemused, as the academic rose up instead. Knowledge was power, and stories almost always came with rules, sometimes strange ones about what could and couldn't be revealed, and to whom. Which meant smart heroines needed to use their brains, not their swords.

She cast back to her latest dream, trying to ignore the awful image of the man with Jamie's face lying bleak and still on a rustic cot, fighting for his life. She needed to see her way to the story underneath. "Tell me about Mirena's mother."

The old siren blinked.

Holly pressed her advantage. "She was given the same choice as Mirena—to sing, or her love would die. What happened?"

A long, strained silence, and then something in Dedra crumbled. The old siren reached out her hand ever so gently and touched an arc of naked bone. "They tell me this is what is left of her."

Holly looked at the skull of what might be her generations-removed great-grandmother and swallowed hard. "How did she end up here? What happened to her?"

"She was pregnant with Mirena, and she chose to live."

That much had been in the dream. "And the man she loved died."

"He did. Not an unusual fate in those days, but she always lived with the guilt. She survived for thirteen years with that agony eating away at her, and then she threw herself off the rocks." Sorrow twisted Dedra's face. "My sisters found her then, and brought her here."

Something bitter and hard and eerily familiar slammed into Holly's gut. "Wait—is that what happened to my mother?" There had always been questions about the accident on the normally quiet stretch of road. Doubts. Whispers they had tried to keep away from her distressed and wildly grieving only daughter.

"I don't know." Dedra's eyes slid partway closed. "We see best when those of our blood stay close to the sea."

Holly remembered an entire summer spent begging to go to the beach. She'd been eight, and enamored with sand castles and mermaids and tales of the creatures under the sea. "She never wanted to go."

"She did once. Stood right on the top of the rocks at Cape Minerva and hurled insults into the water." The old siren's face almost relaxed into a smile. "For someone who didn't know a lot of sailors, she did quite well."

That was impossibly hard to imagine. "I wrote a play once in tenth grade—a monologue where the main character said 'fuck.' She made me take it out before talent night so I wouldn't embarrass her for the rest of eternity."

Blue-gray eyes churned. "Humans have no idea what eternity is."

The piercing exhaustion in those words shoved Holly hard out of memory and into awareness that there were two souls on these forsaken rocks, and the other one had a lot of centuries under her belt.

A millennium of watching women choose—and of watching them die.

A horrible kind of witnessing. The kind of suffering that might leave an old siren with bitter eyes, crackling impatience, and the appearance of a hard heart and shards for a soul.

Holly reached out a hand in Dedra's direction and paused, realizing her perch was far too precarious to make the connection a physical one. Instead, she sought the siren's eyes. "How many have you watched die?"

Tired eyes tried for thousand-year-old steel and didn't quite get there. "Many. Some because they sang and did not sing well enough to join us. Some because they did not sing and killed themselves when their loves died. Some who lived with the guilt for a time before they chose to die." Something hot and anguished rose in her voice. "We couldn't make them all forget."

Holly's anger hesitated, sideswiped by the new addition to the storyline. "What do you mean, make them forget?"

An ancient head tipped down, her hand back on the skull of Mirena's mother. "We try. There is a use of power, of song

—a spell you might call it—that can block memory. It does not work for all. Some love too much, or have too much strength of mind."

There was empathy there, and judgment, and pity for those who had been weak. "Is that what you did for my mother?"

A long silence, filled only by the crashing waves. "Yes. She chose not to sing. I tried to help her forget."

Holly closed her eyes and wondered just how much of her own history she didn't know.

And then she heard a sigh, soft as a baby's breath. She looked up and watched a single tear trace down the old siren's cheek and land in the sea. Sympathy gripped Holly's throat, closing off the words of anger. Dedra was not the evil villain in this story, or evil's messenger. For a thousand years she had fought the curse, even as she was its plaything.

And her fingers, even now, caressed a long-dead skull.

DEDRA COULD SEE the girl's gaze focusing on the skulls, her eyes sharpening. And even though the old siren feared where that could lead, she found that she could not lift her hand away.

This one saw so much.

"Are any of these the skulls of men?" asked Holly quietly.

Anger flashed, driving away some of the harsh sorrow. "You think it is only dead men who deserve to be honored?"

"No." The girl shook her head, eyes solemn. "It's only that I'm afraid to ask my next question."

That was an event that scared them both—and seemed

inevitable now. Dedra waited silently to see if the courage would be found.

"So many? So many women?"

It was the hitching tears in Holly's voice that kept Dedra from speaking the truth. This was only a small fraction, a collection of those most special to her heart. "Some are those who sang and did not give themselves entirely to the sea. Some are my sisters."

"Sisters?"

Dedra realized her sorrow had spoken the word out loud. Oh, how she missed them. Sophia and Cleatris and all who had come before them. She clenched her eyes shut, fighting back the keening lament. There would be time for that later. She met serious brown eyes and spoke between the crashing of the waves. "Even sirens eventually die."

Sorrow—and then more of that questing intellect. "You haven't."

Yet. Sometimes the whisper of death was so strong, Dedra didn't know where she found the strength to resist. "It is sadness that takes them." And guilt. The knowing that there was so very little they could do to stop the pain and death and remembering.

Holly's eyes held horror now. "How many of you are left?"

In a thousand years, no one had ever asked. And Dedra found she didn't have it in her to deny the truth. She squared her shoulders, demanding that the crushing weight rise enough to give her room to breathe. "I am the last."

There was no sound. Even the waves stopped, honoring the truth that now hung over the droplets of cool sea water—or condemning it.

Dedra bowed her head and submitted to their judgment. A

moment of weakness, and perhaps a fatal one. It asked too much of the girl. She wasn't ready.

"You do this alone?" It was a whisper, one from a soul looking on the face of horror—and who found it in her to offer kindness, all the same.

The old siren felt her throat closing. It was not in her power to take away what would come next.

But oh, how her heart wished it.

CHAPTER TWENTY-TWO

*D*aylight. Toddlers pushing grocery carts. The clacks and dings and punctuated conversation of people in a small town filling their pantries for the day or for the week.

Holly stood in the canned-goods aisle of the Foodmart and tried not to shiver.

She'd sought out this place as a bastion of sane and normal, and she didn't plan to leave until most of Holly Castas had soaked in that vibe and landed back on her feet. Preferably with her legs aching a little less than they did at this moment. She put her hands on the cart she'd taken mostly to hold herself up. Ibuprofen was three aisles over—she could at least deal with that basic life need while she was here.

She resolutely grabbed three cans of beans at random as she walked. Her pantry was bare enough that even the mice were likely starving. She snagged a bag of rice, too, the kind that cooked in fifteen minutes and tasted like home. Mom had believed that fixing the demons of hungry, angry, lonely, and tired cured most things, and she hadn't been wrong.

Holly stopped abruptly, squeezing her eyes shut against the sharp pangs that had come out of nowhere. She inhaled, one wavering breath at a time, letting the hurt go on the exhale, keeping her hands wrapped tightly around the shopping cart's sturdy metal bar. It had been a long time since grief had caught her this unaware.

Eleven years ago, it had stalked her daily. Hourly. Stabbing every last attempt she'd made to pull her life together and find some sort of happiness from the torn-up scraps she'd been left with.

She took a last, shuddering breath and opened her eyes. She'd stitched together that life, the one that had felt impossible in the months after her mother died. And now blue-gray eyes were picking at the threads that held the whole thing together.

She grabbed another can of beans and growled. Dedra wasn't the enemy here—she was just a visible target, unlike some amorphous curse that was threatening to upend a good and decent and hard-fought-for life.

Holly knew she deeply needed to talk this out, but nobody sane was going to believe her, especially when she still wasn't sure what she believed herself. Things that made a lot of sense while standing on a wet rock surrounded by skulls seemed far more ephemeral in the solid reality of the canned-goods aisle.

Drama lived here, but not the kind that defied belief.

Holly tried to swallow the dusty grit in her throat and navigated into the next aisle, making her way around two older gentlemen chatting in the baking supplies. They barely paused, even as she wheeled in between their discussion about the merits of adding a little beer to their bread dough.

That almost made her smile. She'd have to pass that tip along to Monster for his pretzels.

She passed by the bread display and pulled a loaf into her cart, a little less randomly this time. She might not bake her own, but she could at least pick something from one of the local bakeries. The other stuff had ingredients that required a chemistry major to understand, and that had always struck her as a little frightening in a food source.

Real life was slowly seeping through the cracks of what was left of Holly Castas. She could feel it landing, just like the weight in her shopping cart.

The dreams were fierce, but they were something entirely different than cans of beans and loaves of bread.

She wasn't, however, prepared to say they weren't real. Not anymore. The evidence was piling up to the point that even the academic was getting nauseous.

She added three bags of chocolate chips to her cart and considered the awful phone call that had chased her out of her apartment like the hordes of hell had landed.

Great-aunt Patrice had married into the family two generations back and taken on their history as if it mattered far more than her own. She was the batty old librarian who had retired and transitioned her genealogy hobby into a full-time obsession. Holly had always been fond of her outrageous stories about long-dead kin, even though she'd assumed most of them had only a passing acquaintance with truth.

One quick phone call—Patrice didn't use email—had been enough to change all that. Holly had asked if there were any tales of untimely death buried in the family tree, hoping to discover that everyone had died in their sleep at the ripe old age of a hundred and three. Instead, she'd been regaled with her great-aunt's long list of the morbid and the bizarre.

So many accidents. So many unexplained deaths. Ancestors simply disappearing off the face of the genealogical earth. Patrice thought it a great mystery. Holly was horribly afraid she might know why.

The deaths hadn't been on the main trunk of the tree, the one that followed the male line. They'd been on the sprouts and branches—the offshoot limbs created when Patrice had been able to trace back one of their female relations. Holly was pretty sure that a family tree of her female ancestors would show an awful pattern of dead young women and the men they loved.

She'd been too soul sick to ask Patrice to try. Some evidence wasn't something a human heart could bear in black and white.

Holly's eyes squeezed shut again, wondering exactly what had taken her mother's life. They'd had such a rocky relationship, and maybe now she had some ideas about why. There was just no way this curse was easy on those left living, either. And she had no idea what to do about that.

The stakes felt so very damn high.

Was she condemned to a life of not loving so she might end up like her great-aunt, alive and well and slightly batty?

The alternative was being accessory to murder.

Holly shuddered, wishing that sounded overly melodramatic—and remembered she'd come to the Foodmart to get away from exactly that. She needed better fodder than family ghosts and the skulls of long-lost ancestors if she wanted to stay sane. Time to get some sausages, something that passed for fruit-and-vegetable servings, and bust out of this place. She'd already lost one day of work to this mess, and the Haversham powers-that-be would notice if she kept that up.

She'd made it safely around a five-year-old manning a shopping cart with a maniac glint in his eye, and a little old lady surveying cake mixes, when running footsteps caught her attention. They were far too loud to be a Foodmart ghost.

She turned and saw Monster slide to a stop, clutching his phone, eyes bleak and worried and ramping up to frantic.

Holly grabbed his hands, none too gently. "What's wrong?" She knew nothing about his family, but this had the look of that kind of tragedy about it.

He met her eyes and swallowed. "It's Jamie. He's been hit by a car."

She could feel all her blood go to wherever Monster's had fled. Her head swam, everything hitting that surreal place that comes when people you know are dead and dying. "What? How?"

Monster's hands started to shake. "He pulled over to help a couple on the side of the road on his way back from the city. Someone lost control and hit all three of them. Jamie was the only one seriously hurt." He closed his eyes and wheezed in the breath of an eighty-year-old asthmatic. "He's in a coma."

Holly fought back the surreal fog. "Where is he? I'll take you there." Probably neither of them should be driving, but she could at least keep her eyes open.

"They took him to the city. To intensive care." Monster fished in his jeans for his keys, and then just stood looking at them like a small boy who'd found a dead tadpole in his pocket.

She took them gently out of his hands. Clearly this had hit

him with the force of a sledgehammer. "You guys are really tight, huh?"

"Yeah. We grew up on the same street, and his parents let me stay at their place a lot when my family didn't have their shit together."

Holly pulled him toward the doors of the grocery store, acutely aware that she knew nothing of Monster's history. He'd just always been a part of the Inkspot's scenery.

She herded him toward his truck, trying to avoid the haunted look on his pale face. It reminded her far too much of Mirena, sitting at Mikel's bedside.

CHAPTER TWENTY-THREE

*S*tage makeup had nothing on the real thing.

That was the inane thought, the only thought in Holly's mind as she stared at the impossibly pale face on the white hospital pillow.

Monster had gotten them into the intensive care room with the expedient statement that he was Jamie's brother. Judging from the way the two wan, older people standing on the other side of the bed had reacted when he'd shown up, it probably wasn't far from the truth.

If love mattered, if love could help Jamie recover, all he needed was right around this bed.

Holly gulped, well aware she was just a stage prop for this particular scene. Maybe she could get everyone something to eat. Or chairs—Jamie's dad looked like he might fall over any minute, and the staunch, sturdy woman at his side couldn't hold him up forever.

She moved one step backward, two. She didn't belong here.

Her eyes cast around, looking for other things she might be able to do to help. To distance. To escape.

Her eyes fell on the name in big, bold letters at the top of his chart. Jamie Mikel Cadavell.

She felt her breath hissing. "His middle name is Mikel?"

Monster looked at her like she'd grown snake hair. "Yeah. Named after some great-grandfather or something."

The awful possibility she'd been holding at bay through sheer brute force broke through the dam of her denial and flooded everything it touched. Reasonable doubt, academic skepticism, common sense—all drowned in the bone-deep certainty that somehow an ancient curse had reached down through the millennia and run a car into the body of a man who grew spinach for a living.

Holly lurched out into the hospital hallway, Jamie's white face seared in her mind and the rampaging elephants of denial trampling all coherent thought in her skull.

This couldn't be happening.

This was just evil coincidence intersecting badly with a week of stress and tension and overactive dreams. It wasn't Mikel lying in that room, not her beloved, and she wasn't some village girl with adoration in her heart and a story dragged out of mythological nightmare.

Sirens, whatever else they might be, weren't blood-and-bones real. They were archetypes, larger-than-life embodiments of something fundamentally important to humanity's collective truth. But sirens weren't real, and they weren't cursed, and she didn't come from a long line of women who had met horrible destinies under the light of the full moon.

Her heart pounded with the frantic beat of denial.

She was Holly Isadore Castas, a thirty-year-old academic

who wrote dusty papers and occasionally dressed herself in princess frocks for fun. She wasn't the kind of person who faced down the powers of life and death. There were plenty of other explanations for what was going on, and while most of them ended with her locked up in a ward somewhere, getting close and personal with a cup full of little white pills, they beat being responsible for what lay in that hospital room.

So white. So still.

Holly careened off the walls of the corridor and circled back from whence she'd come. Her feet didn't have any more idea of how to handle this than her head did.

She threw herself into the nearest puke-green plastic chair and drew her knees up under her chin. Hot tears formed behind her scrunched-up eyelids. Jamie had been so still. She didn't have to be his soul mate to feel the sucky, hovering threat of that.

People died every day, even people she loved.

There had never been anything she could do about it, and warped dreams that were trying to convince her otherwise were just a really torturous form of wish fulfillment.

She didn't want this. She didn't want to be here seeing the wan, comatose face of a guy who had just started getting interesting enough to matter, and wondering what the hell she was supposed to do. This wasn't a role she had auditioned for, and if the curtains were about to go up, she had no earthly idea what her lines were.

The tears hit her jeans-clad knees and soaked in, hot and itchy and not nearly voluminous enough to speak of the anguish kicking inside her.

There had been no tears around that bedside. Dry faces

and eyes that had somehow figured out how to replace terror with love.

Holly scrubbed her cheeks with the backs of her hands and stood up, sniffling. She didn't love the man on the bed like they did, and sitting out here pulling out her hair and rending her clothing didn't serve anyone. If they could be brave and stalwart and true—and every molecule of her believed that mattered—the least she could do was to bring them sandwiches and chairs and whatever else might support the performance they were putting on for their audience of one.

It was her turn to be the props master.

CHAPTER TWENTY-FOUR

*H*olly stumbled in the door of her apartment, exhausted down to her toenails. The nurses in intensive care had finally swept her, none too gently, out of their ward and told her not to come back until she'd had some sleep.

Jamie's parents had been sequestered somewhere they put people who were actually related. Monster was still standing quiet guard on a wall in Jamie's room—the nurses had taken one look at his determined bulk and let him be.

Holly had made him eat a slice of pizza—most of one, anyhow. And fetched coffee and chairs and headache meds and generally tried to keep the universe from falling apart, one trip to the hospital cafeteria at a time.

Now she was home and there was nothing left but to let the pieces of Holly Castas crumble.

"No way, girlfriend." The hand at her back could have given lessons to the nurses. "There's a really comfortable bed in ten more steps and we're getting you into it, even if I have to drag you."

Given how much weight she had on Jade, it would be plain mean to make her keep that promise. Holly drew in a shuddering breath and willed her feet to keep moving. She debated between the couch and her bed, and took the left turn that would bring her to the latter.

Sleep was definitely coming very soon on the agenda, but not the rest-and-recuperate kind. Exhaustion never got even the most bumbling heroines off the hook, not in any story worth the air to tell it. She had no idea how Holly Castas had managed to get herself cast in this particular role, but all evidence said she had, or at least enough evidence that she couldn't possibly ignore it. Not with a man's life riding on the gamble. Which meant there was a battle to fight, even tired and road weary and heartsick as she was.

Just as soon as she figured out where to swing her sword. She'd called Jade for a ride home for more than one reason.

Holly sank into her bed, piteously relieved by the flamboyant bedspread and mismatched pillows. Color lived here. Life.

Bumbling warriors took sustenance wherever they could find it.

Jade sat down beside her, eyes worried. "Can you stay awake long enough for me to heat you up some soup or something?"

That had been left in her abandoned shopping basket at the Foodmart. "There's peanut butter. I think."

Her best friend snorted. "You think I mean food from your cupboard?" She hefted the huge backpack that had been slung over her shoulder. "I know you. I came prepared. Tuck your-self in, and I'll be back with victuals in a second."

When someone studied the Middle Ages, that might mean a fairly wide range of foodstuffs, but Holly was too tired to care. She managed to strip off her pants, and decided the rest was close enough to pajamas to leave in place.

Whatever energy she had left needed to be routed to her brain.

In what felt like mere moments later, she felt the unmis-takable tilt of another body landing on the bed next to her, followed quickly by the kind of smells that had her nose ready to sit up and beg.

Holly levered one eye open.

"Pho," said Jade, setting down her tray and pointing at the bowl of soup. "Nicely spicy, but not suicidal. Sweet potato chili, ham and cheese croissant, pork egg rolls. Pick your poison."

It was a multicultural buffet. "You had all this sitting in your fridge?"

"Yeah." Jade pushed a small container of sauce a little closer to the egg rolls. "International student potluck at my place on Friday night."

Her best friend had run that group when they'd been undergrads. Now she just acted as their benevolent auntie. It was a good gig for everyone—the sometimes lonely and out-of-place students who had landed from countries far and wide, and the woman who had extra care-taking genes and a vast interest in the world and all its differences.

Holly reached for the egg rolls. Those she could eat with her fingers. She wasn't sure she had enough dexterity left to try a soup spoon. "Thank you."

"No problem at all." The words were quiet, deeply meant, and edged with concern. "Want to talk about it?"

She didn't, but she needed to, and she needed Jade's rock-solid brain and heart to be the ones listening.

Every twenty-first-century instinct Holly had said that it was entirely impossible that Jamie was lying in a hospital bed because of some ancient curse, and it was beyond belief that Holly Castas came from a bloodline which had paid the price of said curse for hundreds or thousands of years. But there was too much evidence piling up to ignore, at least if you were a story-analyzing academic who happily took evidence with several grains of salt.

Scientists were different. Jade was gorgeous and loyal and fantastic in every possible way, but she would never put her life on the line for the contents of a dream.

Holly dipped an egg roll in as much sweet plum sauce as it could possibly hold and popped it in her mouth. She chewed, letting the sweet, rich goo blend with the crispy wrapper and its deep-fried pork innards.

Battle food.

She kept eating, working her way through the entire plate of egg rolls, letting the salty and sweet and fried fortify her.

And when she finally felt the beginnings of new energy flowing into her veins, she looked over into the worried eyes of her best friend and started filling her in on the details. The continued dreams. The chats with Dedra, the last siren, with only skulls left to love. A mother's pendant and a deadly family tree. A medieval rockslide. Mikel's pale, unconscious face and Mirena's heartsick one.

Jade listened, quietly spooning in sweet-potato-studded chili and saying absolutely nothing.

Holly's fingers wrapped around her pendant. Somewhere between the coffee runs and the look of love in Jamie's mother's eyes, she'd pieced together the meaning of her strange birthday gift of long ago. "I think Mom wanted this to protect me. To remind the curse she'd already made the sacrifice." Total speculation, but it felt right. It just hadn't worked.

Holly took a deep breath and connected the last dots. "And it's not just my family history. When I was in the hospital, I saw Jamie's chart. His middle name is Mikel."

"Ah." Jade spoke at last, and when she did, it was a single word.

Holly waited. For reassurances that this was not real, that it wasn't her fault, that the parallels were only the product of a fevered mind and tragic coincidence.

Instead, strong, slim fingers reached out to take her hand. "What are you going to do?"

Holly blinked. She'd needed perspective, to get out of the swirling, dangerous fog of mythology and into real life. Jade was a pragmatic, catapult-building, fungus-growing scientist.

And somehow, she was landing on the side of story.

Jade shrugged and raised an eyebrow. "What? My ancestors carved fertility masks that still freak me out when I'm ovulating. You didn't think I could swallow this?"

Holly still wasn't sure *she* could. "You really think I'm caught up in some old curse? That life and death rides on what I do next?"

"I don't know, but if there's a chance it might, you gotta do something. And I think you know that already."

She'd been hoping for a scientific Hail Mary. Being cast as Dedra's replacement sucked on every level possible. Holly wrapped her arms around her ribs and swallowed hard. "I keep hoping there's a way out."

"Yeah." Jade leaned back, eyes thoughtful. "You know, this sounds a bit like a boardroom negotiation. Plenty of those feel like life and death too—or at least, people act as if they are."

That was the last place Holly had expected this conversation to go. Her best friend talked about her family background exactly never. "What, so I should wear a suit and wield a really dangerous laser pointer when I traipse off to sing?"

Jade's lips quirked up. "Not unless you want to look really stupid. But war is war—the trappings don't matter so much."

Which might be why her favorite catapult builder spent so much time studying medieval battlefield strategy. Holly's brain was getting in gear now. "How do you win? In one of those boardroom deals?" Or on a Middle Age battlefield, for that matter. Warfare wasn't her turf—she only studied the songs and stories people made up after the fighting was done.

"You collect power," said Jade quietly, eyes deadly serious. "You shake things up—modify the terms of the deal, or where the fight happens, or what everyone has to eat for breakfast. Change the rules, make them yours, get better information than everyone else."

That was easier said than done. "I tried that already." She glared at the stack of books on her bedside table—they'd totally failed her on this one.

Jade followed her gaze. "Knowledge is power, but it doesn't all come from books, girlfriend."

"Heretic."

"Realist."

Holly wobbled on her last exhausted neuron and begged it to keep the lights on. "So if you were in one of those boardroom brawls and you needed better information, how would you get it?"

"If you're my father—spies, threats, and bribes."

Those didn't sound very applicable. Holly painstakingly dunked another egg roll. "And if you're not?"

Jade smiled. "If you're Holly Castas and you've made friends with the locals, you go back and talk to them."

Her last neuron managed a weak ping. "Dedra."

"Yeah." Jade's eyes carried something darker now. Fiercer. "You have a source for info. Use her. You want to win a war, you need to learn from the ones who succeeded. The ones who didn't end up roadkill. Go talk to your siren, and this time, take your brain with you."

Holly blinked. It hadn't ever been hard to imagine her best friend pulling the levers of corporate power one day—but this version of Jade could pull them ruthlessly.

It ran in her blood.

Just like Holly had an inheritance running in hers.

CHAPTER TWENTY-FIVE

*H*olly looked down at her bare toes, clenching sand that had become all too familiar, and willed the siren to be on the rocks inside the cove when she looked up. If it was at all in her control, she planned to stay dry this time, and well away from the skulls of her long-dead relations.

She had a different kind of genealogy to wield tonight.

She kept her head bowed a moment longer, and then raised her eyes, staring out into the icy moonlight.

Dedra waited silently on the nearby rocks.

Holly bit her lower lip and let her breath go fast and hard. She didn't have enough energy left for this to go slowly. She needed to collect power. New rules, better knowledge. "What was your name? Before?"

She saw shock pass across the old siren's eyes, followed briefly by denial—and then relief. Dedra sat, still as glass, her gaze never leaving Holly's face.

A geyser of empathy fountained in Holly's ribs, for the

young kitchen girl and the tough, lonely old woman she had become. "You were Mirena, weren't you?"

Blue-gray eyes closed, and stayed that way for a long time. When Dedra spoke again, her voice wavered. "My name has been Dedra for a thousand years. Before that, I was a young and foolish girl by the name of Mirena, who loved Mikel." The old siren opened her eyes. "No one has ever asked that before."

"In a thousand years?" Holly scowled—she didn't want to be descended from a long line of idiots.

Something that almost passed for a smile lit in Dedra's eyes. "The ones who came before you didn't lack in intelligence, girl. Not all of them, anyhow."

A thousand years was a long time for everyone to miss the obvious—and a long time for some other things, too. Holly looked at the fierce old siren and wondered just what a millennium of grief had wrought. "You sang. And Mikel lived."

A slow nod.

Holly looked beyond the tough outer shell, seeking the love-struck girl who might still live within. "You saved him."

A single tear slid down a salt-stained cheek, one that bore witness to the entire, awful weight of that choice.

Holly bowed her head again, this time acknowledging. Honoring.

Dedra stirred, tail restive. "That isn't what you came here to ask."

It wasn't—and the brusque words yanked Jamie's pale face back into clear focus. Holly dipped her chin again, gathering her courage. "I came to ask for a singing lesson."

When she looked up this time, Dedra was gaping.

Somehow, that caught Holly as funny. "What, has no one asked that in a thousand years either?"

A fierce head shook slowly, looking almost befuddled.

Change the rules. Collect power. Jade's words resonated in Holly's head. Maybe this wasn't so different from corporate wheeling and dealing after all. She kept her eyes glued to the one woman she was absolutely sure had looked this curse squarely in the eyes and won. "What happened to Mikel?"

Dedra shrugged quietly. "He lived a long, happy life. He had four children. Two sons, two daughters."

With someone else.

DEDRA COULD FEEL IT NOW, the geysering grief she'd spent centuries tamping down—and spewing into the atmosphere along with it, a vast ocean of feelings. Horror and loneliness, terrible rage, aching joy.

She had saved Mikel and his descendants. They had lived simple, often happy, normal lives. Jamie lived in this time because Mirena had wielded the full power of her choice and her song and the wild depths of a foolish girl's love.

Mirena had saved Mikel's line—and Dedra had protected hers as best as she could ever since. Even a siren's song wasn't enough to break the curse, but it kept it leashed. Limited. Shackled, so that those of her line and his—most of them, anyhow—could live the lives they'd been meant for.

And now the curse stalked her and Mikel's bloodlines both.

The wondrous, questing, brave young woman in front of her should not have to do this. Everything in Dedra that had once shrieked and railed against the injustice of the world rose up again, as volcanic as it had ever been. There must be a way to end this.

There must be a way.

She stared fiercely into the eyes of the only daughter who might be able to do it—the one who had come to request a singing lesson, of all things—and made her own choice. If this girl, named so incongruously for a pretty red berry, could stand and fight, she would do it with everything a thousand years of knowledge and will and perilously eked survival could give her.

Holly was staring at her, eyes wide.

Dedra felt her first real smile in centuries forming. "Never underestimate the power of a really old woman, my dear."

The girl blinked. "I can see that."

It was time they both stepped into the full power of who they were, for Holly to discover the full truth of what ran in her blood, and for an old siren to stop being a frail, helpless, withered shell.

"Here is what I know." Dedra reached for what had saved Mikel's life and drenched her words with the truth of it. "You will sing life into Jamie through your love."

Holly winced. "He's a really nice guy, but it hasn't gone there yet."

Foolish modern ideas of romance. "You must sing as if it has." And that was the easy part. Dedra waited for the indecisive muck to leave the girl's face—this was not the time to coddle her. That time might well never come again. "But if you want to live as well, you must do more."

Desperate uncertainty flared in the girl's eyes.

Dedra cursed. "You will not live as a woman. But if you

sing well enough, you will join me in these waters." For as long as an old siren could hold on, anyhow. She would not willingly leave a young sister alone—she knew far too well the agony of that loneliness.

Holly took a slow, wavering breath. "I don't know if I want that."

Dedra closed her eyes and willed her own desperate need out of them. In this she would leave the girl as much choice as she was able. On the scales of fate, the need of a tired old woman for companionship weighed less than a speck of dust.

It was one of the very few things she could give. "That choice will be yours."

Holly gulped. "If I decide I do…" Her voice trailed off.

Dedra closed her eyes against the panic. The girl would find the strength to do this. She must. "You will sing the song of his heart and call him to life. And then you will sing the song of your own heart—and if you are true enough to all of who you can and will be, you will join me here."

And perhaps together they could keep the curse fettered a few centuries more.

The girl looked puzzled and so terribly uncertain.

One more time, Dedra dug for patience—and for the unlikely wisdom she had found in a dusty corner of a young kitchen girl's heart. "You must be brave enough to look at all of who you are, and then you must insist that you have a right to continue being."

"But not as the human person I am now." Holly's eyes were flat, her voice hard.

The old siren welcomed any and all signs the girl had backbone. She would need it. "I am far more aware than you are of the inequities of this curse."

A soft, embarrassed sigh. "Of course you are."

Dedra remembered the eyes of the three who had come to her in the moonlit cove so many eons ago, how they had looked at her when she had awoken in the shallows of the small cave that was her first siren memory. With welcome, and longing, and surging regret.

They had not been kind—they'd known that would break her. But they had sat on distant rocks for months and listened to her furious, lashing, unrelenting lament.

It was that energy she would will now to the daughter of her blood.

"I won't ask you to help me find a way out," said Holly abruptly. "I assume that if you're here, there isn't one, at least that you know of."

Something in Dedra rejoiced at the spirit in that final caveat, and recoiled at its content. This was a fate that must be fully, entirely accepted, and searching for an exit door was a sign of both good common sense—and terribly dangerous denial. "Hundreds before you have tried to find one. They all failed." She would not kill hope, but she wouldn't fan it to life, either. "I know only that you must be strong, and you must give all of yourself to your song, even the parts you wish could be hidden away."

"Full self-expression." Holly's eyes had gone oddly opaque. "The stories of sirens, they speak of you singing a song so beautiful that men can't turn away."

Dedra managed to hold on to her temper—something in the girl's question wasn't aiming at the usual idiocy. "All human souls are drawn to a heart that knows itself. Those who are most lost can't turn away." She swallowed a sudden, unbidden lump in her throat. "Not only men."

Horrified understanding dawned in Holly's eyes. "You have to sing. To continue to exist, you have to keep singing. And when you do, sometimes people die."

The old siren had waited a thousand years for someone to understand this well. And now that someone had, she had the fiercest urge to sweep the girl off to some tiny cove no human eyes had ever found and guard her brightness. "With every choice you make, people will die."

There was no way to protect everyone, especially the soul of courage and light standing in front of her. Dedra sighed and fanned her tail once, pushing herself back into deeper waters.

It was time to show the girl the end.

CHAPTER TWENTY-SIX

*H*olly felt herself thrashing, fighting the messages of dream. Willing herself to remember them. Pleading with the universe to forget.

She didn't want this to be her fight. Her death.

The dark tugged her back under.

She felt the tears welling up.

She didn't want to see.

THE CHOICE, in the end, was not a hard one.

The hard part was accepting that she had to make it, and Tirenne had accomplished that with a few short words.

Mirena stood at the edge of the waters and clutched the pendant to her heart, weeping for the father she had never known, the woman who had loved him and carried the guilt of his death every day of the rest of her life, and for the next generation the curse would harm.

Because she knew well what the unearthly trio had not. This would scar Mikel. Their love had the solid feel of something that lasted the tests of time. He would go on, because no one knew better than a farmer that planting needed to come after death. But he would mourn her, and something in his gentle, contented steadiness would never be the same again.

Or she was just a foolish girl who wanted to believe that she lived that deeply in his heart.

In the end, it mattered not, for he lived that deeply in hers, and she would do what was necessary to keep him as safe as she could. If the brigands got him after that, she would figure out how to sing herself into a terrible wind and suck their souls from their bodies.

Somehow, the idea of that made her feel better.

Mirena bowed her head and took a step forward, letting the cool waters lap at her bare feet, catch the hem of her dress.

It was Mikel's favorite.

She had to believe that this price she was about to pay would earn him a long and happy life, one that would hold the usual portions of sorrow, but not the sharp knives of war or sickness or early death. She would sing of it, just as the women in the waters had told her. The very best of her hopes and dreams and her love for him.

She reached the rocks close in to shore, and as she stood by them, looking out at the crashing seas beyond the cove, her confidence wavered.

She was a kitchen girl with a voice that carried a tune well enough for scrubbing pots, but that was all. Even in her small village there were far prettier singers, and in the summer months, traveling minstrels and bards wandered down the road almost every week. Surely there was someone far more able to sing Mikel the kind of life he deserved.

A small voice whispered the answer even as she thought it. There was no one who loved him as much as she did, and he was only a tenant farmer, with not even a small plot of land to his name yet.

He mattered to her as he did to no one else.

She was the only one who could see the Mikel she saw in her dreams. The one with prosperous fields and a warm fire lit all through the winter and children who gathered at his side with bellies full of bread and stew and happiness in their eyes. The family he would plant with workmanlike care and tend with his big, gentle, uncommonly wise hands.

It wasn't the water she saw now. It was Mikel, an old man of fifty winters with his family gathered round, snug in the house built with his own hands. The youngest of the babes would be tucked in the crook of his arm, dwarfed by muscles still used to long, hard work in the fields. He would look down at his sleeping grandson and run a finger down his nose, just like he did with her when she'd done something that amused him.

And his eyes would be filled with the deep contentment of one who had lived a long and good life.

She did not sing to the water this night, or to the creatures who waited somewhere in the deep beyond, or to the moon, or to her sore and trembling heart. She would sing to Mikel. To the man he was now, and the man he would become.

Even without her.

The first notes of her song floated out softly over the water, barely heard over the small, polite waves of the cove. It didn't matter. Mikel had never been a loud man, or one of those hard of hearing. If he could hear small green shoots growing in spring, he could hear this.

Her legs steadied under her, bare feet digging into the soft sand under her toes. She'd meant to stand on the rocks, but that wasn't right either. Her love was a man who dug into the ground, and she wanted her last memories of this world to be ones with softness under her feet.

Her song strengthened, wordless sounds that somehow knew how to join one to the next. There was no pattern to them, nothing like the familiar choruses the minstrels used to get people clapping their hands and dropping coins into the cup by the fire.

This was music that would only be sung once.

Tears rolled down her cheeks as she felt power rising within her. Whatever witchery this was, whatever magic, it was strong.

Strong enough to save a man's life.

Strong enough to make it a good one.

Her eyes still locked on the old man with the contented smile sitting by the fire, she sang of all that she'd imagined for the two of them. Nights on a blanket under the moon where she might discover what it was that made people laugh at the bawdier ballads. Pain welcomed, and a baby's cry. Laughing little ones splashing in a mud puddle between the field rows, or bending down to push seeds into the soil under Mikel's careful watch.

He would have all those things. Even the curses of the gods only had a right to steal so much.

She was nearing the end now, her spirit poured out, sacrificed so that a good man might have a good life. Mirena held the last wavering notes and looked one last time into the eyes of the man she had sung them to.

Looked—and said good-bye.

Then, sinking down into the embrace of the cool, wet sand and the encroaching waters, she let go.

Let the darkness come. The deep, cold nothingness.

And then the three.

Holding her as she floated on the undulating waves.

Greeting her. Welcoming her.

Sharing her terrible grief.

The sisterhood of rended hearts.

HOLLY WOKE UP WEEPING, the image of the three and the one who joined them pouring a scorching waterfall of tears out of her eyes. Great hurtling, choking sobs, the kind she'd shed in the entirely creepy cemetery where they'd lowered her mother into a hole in the ground and covered the last remnants of normal life as she knew it with shovels full of dirt.

Holly shuddered, immersed still in the pure, sheer bravery in every note of Mirena's song.

She could not sing such a song for Jamie—she knew that now. She didn't have enough dreams, not ones soaked in the kind of love that was necessary to make them real. She would have to find something else to sing of instead.

If she could.

Mirena's choice had been both far harder and far easier.

171

Holly would have to find a different way, a different path, a different power—or walk away from them and pray for a different ending. She could only hope that whatever she chose, she could find the tiniest part of Mirena's raw, sublime bravery.

The courage of a woman singing herself to death.

CHAPTER TWENTY-SEVEN

*H*olly sat in a small flowered courtyard just outside the emergency room doors of the hospital where Jamie lay, still and white, some vital part of him lost or deeply sleeping.

She had somehow needed to be close while she fought the ghosts of dream and story and her own heart.

She wasn't Mirena. It had taken most of the morning and several very strong cups of coffee to get a grip on that, but she wasn't a medieval kitchen girl, she wasn't a woman deep in love, and she wasn't a child who had grown up deeply connected to ocean waters and the cycles of the moon.

Her beliefs ran deep, but they ran different.

This whole turn of the story was running different. The man in peril this time wasn't her beloved. What ran in Holly's veins when she thought of Jamie was interesting, but magnitudes different from who Mirena and Mikel were for each other.

Dedra was convinced that the stakes hadn't changed, that

the curse had her in its sights. Given the timing of Jamie's collision with a moving vehicle, it was hard to take a firm stand against that. A curse that had just gotten a whole lot crazier could still be a curse. It wouldn't be the first time dementia had woven itself into a storyline.

Holly hugged her knees. Even her neat, academic brain couldn't fight off the hideous conviction that Jamie was in deep danger because he happened to have gotten close enough to her to trigger an ancient energy's net.

That, and his middle name. She wasn't the only one with history running in her veins.

She could believe the two of them had fallen into the gravitational well of the curse. But it was a big step from there to being willing to give up her life for a man she was just beginning to know.

Maybe she should go see him again. Look on the pale face and the stark white sheets and give herself an awful, jolting reminder of the stakes.

Mirena had sat by Mikel's bedside for long days and even longer nights.

Holly reached down and yanked up a droopy orange flower.

She wasn't Mirena. She was Holly Castas, an academic who studied stories, did a pretty good rendition of a whiny fairy princess, and lived far enough from the ocean that it had never made much of an impression on her life.

She stared at the uprooted flower, well aware she wasn't someone who usually destroyed plant life, either.

And then she breathed in, long and slow and deep, and gave oxygen to the idea she'd been trying to grab hold of all morning. She wasn't Mirena—and maybe that wasn't an accident. She had different strengths, different beliefs, a different relationship with the guy at death's door.

Maybe that wasn't because of curse dementia at all.

If none of those things were accidental—and in the best stories, they never were—those differences mattered deeply.

They weren't the weakness of this tale.

They would be where she would find her power.

Holly was on her feet now, pacing wildly through the flowers like a diva who had just found her hook into the role of a lifetime.

She couldn't sing for love, not in the way Mirena had. This wasn't a matter of throwing on a too-small corset and trying to impersonate a princess. She couldn't fake that kind of devotion—her acting skills just weren't that good.

And if Mirena's song had taught her anything, it was that intent mattered.

She needed to find some. Something that she could believe in as fervently, as passionately, as completely as a young kitchen girl singing so that her love might live.

Holly tipped her head up to the sun, took a deep breath, and felt the levitating anger billowing right underneath it. For the first time all morning, she didn't swallow it down. She sucked in the slightly desperate aroma of flowers that lived on the edge of life and death, and dove into her own fury and what it knew.

And found the first of the intentions that she needed.

It was time for this curse to end, to move forward as myth and memory and erode in the sands of time.

It was time for women to stop dying. That, she could get passionately, completely behind.

She felt her storytelling analyst jittering—that wasn't how the curse worked. She sang, or he died. Rules were rules.

Holly pushed her fury at the doubt. She wasn't Mirena. She was a woman a thousand years later, faced with a different set of circumstances, and she was darn well going to come to this fight with different weapons. Carefully, because the story still had to run its course. But if anyone knew how to dance with a story and make it her own, it was the woman who dissected mythology in her day job and brought it to life in her weekend passion.

Holly turned to look at the bland beige hospital brick wall, and the sound that came out of her throat was almost a growl.

Maybe—just maybe—there was a way through this.

CHAPTER TWENTY-EIGHT

S he had no oceans, no favorite seaside rocks, not even a beach she remembered as a child. But Holly knew the place where she needed to sing, even if generations of sirens would roll over in their briny graves.

Change the playing field. Collect her power.

She was fighting this battle on her turf. With fingers chilled by the oddly cool evening breeze and the nerves pounding inside her, she unlocked the door of the Inkspot theater, pulled it open, and breathed in.

This was her salty air. Here, where she smelled the odor of possibility and belief. Here, where she could be anyone and had years of practice demanding that her audience believe, even if the costumes didn't quite fit and the props occasionally lost a limb and the heartthrob's three kids sat in the front row cheering on their dad.

She pulled in a shaky breath. Instead of a small sea of friendly faces and curious onlookers, tonight she performed for an ancient curse and one very old kitchen girl.

Because Holly had a plan, one constructed during the shaky, meandering drive from hospital to theater. A story, one she planned to sell to her audience with every bit of talent and skill and belief she had.

And an ending.

She breathed in of the theater, and of memory. Of her own lived experience. Of lifting a good life out of the rubble and dust of her mother's death. Of finding treasure and everyday drama in the canned-goods aisle of the Foodmart. Of sharing her office with a woman who had somehow convinced a corporate empire to let her study medieval biology instead of going to business school.

Holly made her way slowly toward the stage, a processional of one, letting the shadows and dust motes speak to her. Memories lived here in the Inkspot too. Strength and power to pour into who she already was.

The words of the young sirens to Mirena hammered in her head.

If you don't sing, he will die. If you sing, he will live. If you sing well enough, you will become one of us.

There was truth there, she believed that absolutely now. But sometimes the words weren't the whole truth—they were merely guideposts. Hints to what lay deeper. She'd spent the last eight years of her life dedicated to that kind of parsing, to that kind of digging for the layers of meaning underneath.

Today, lives hung in the balance—and she was about to stake it all on her own personal distillation of the sirens' words. To accept fully the insane idea that her voice carried the power of life and death, and that it could shape what life meant.

Quietly moving to center stage, Holly let the music of her

heart and soul rise up her chest and out into the empty Inkspot theater. The song felt more confident this time— more aware of its own power.

She kept it well in check. This story was going to have a slow build, one that had all the small pieces that would matter woven into its fabric. She let a pretty riff of notes go—a dare, almost—and called academic Holly to the stage.

On this, Dedra was absolutely right. Today wouldn't get done unless all of Holly Castas showed up, and part of what she needed to boss this curse around was an academic's trained and rigorous brain.

She breathed deep into diaphragm and conviction and intent, and sang her hypothesis out into the dusty dark. Things were changing. Sirens had once numbered enough to be counted in waters off a dozen nations, and now there remained just one. The academic only had hints as to why— women who no longer believed enough to sing in the first place, or weren't soaked enough in a culture of story to have faith in the mythology they could become. Questions it was too late to ask, but it fit with what she knew of the modern world's weakening of beliefs of so many kinds.

Some of those losses, Holly grieved deeply—but weakening brought more than death, more than loss. It brought vulnerability. Opportunity.

If mermaids and sirens and archetypes and mythology could evolve over thousands of years, so could curses. Dedra accepted the curse simply as it was, and that made sense—she had given her life to it, seen her bloodline decimated, watched her sisters rise in new form and then die of unfathomable helplessness.

Holly sang to the grandmothers of her line, and to the

mothers and sisters lost. They were a part of this story, in their being and in their dying.

And then academic Holly rang out her surest notes. The ones where her belief ran different.

If modern times and lack of belief had weakened the power of sirens, they would have weakened the curse too. Given it cracks. Perhaps it was one of those cracks that had caused the curse to pick a target this time around who did not yet love. Who had not yet given her heart to her beloved.

Because Holly could see so clearly now, in the dust and the dark. This story was about far more than just Jamie, about far more than whether one man lived or died—and she might be the first one in a thousand years who wasn't blinded by her own love.

Her song was building now. She could feel it rising into the fullness of the story she wanted to tell, of the story she wanted to *be*. Holly smiled as a particularly wild riff sent shivers all up and down her body.

Academic Holly had landed her blows. Now it was time for her heart to speak.

She wasn't Jamie's love, and she wasn't prepared to stand here and sing as if she were. But she was a woman who absolutely believed in his right to live as he chose, to find who he was meant to be, to put the unique energy of Jamie Cadavell out into the universe. To live his story.

She deeply believed in her own right to do that too. It might involve sandpapering some corners, but she had the right to sandpaper the ones she wanted.

Her notes flew into the farthest corners, reaching the ears of the most hidden motes of dust. Tonight she was going to sandpaper the heck out of an ancient curse.

The details of the story were window dressing, always window dressing. Influenced by culture, by oral tradition that didn't always pass things down entirely accurately, by what had happened to the storyteller on the way to dinner.

Stories got sandpapered all the time.

This time she intended to be the one wielding the sandpaper. What ran in her blood made her far more than just a pawn.

Holly tipped her head back and blasted a run of pure energy up to the ceiling. And then she smiled, and using the sounds of her throat and the most preciously held beliefs of her heart, began to pick apart the threads of a very old story and reweave them. To shape a new container from the materials of the old—and to do it with the dexterity and skill of the academic who knew all the pieces of a story and the actress who knew how to put them together into something believable and real, no matter how shabby some of the tools of her trade. A container shaped by the music of her convictions, the ones gathered from the strange, eclectic, and good life of one Holly Castas.

Her gathering of the very personal magic she would use to rewrite the ending.

She only needed one last ingredient.

The curse's truest believer.

Demand streaming from every cell of her body, Holly reached out to Dedra. The old siren swam into view, confused and resistant, hiding her eyes from the brightness, from the light.

Holly insisted, with only the power of her voice, that Dedra look. That she hear.

That she consider the possibility that there was another way.

———

THIS WAS NOT a place of power. There was no water, no rock, no sense of time and tide, no touch of moon or sun.

Dedra felt herself cowering. Nothing about this was right. It offended every mote of who she was, right down to the tattered, see-through remnants of a foolish kitchen girl.

And yet.

She closed her eyes, and bade her ears to listen, because as fiercely alien and wrong as this place was, the power of the song was impossible to deny. Holly sang like no one had sung in five hundred years or more, full of conviction and belief and passion and the strength necessary to pass through to the waters and become a sister.

Finally, after all the waiting, one worthy of joining her had arrived.

And she was singing the wrong song.

Dedra's heart quaked. She didn't have enough will, enough strength, enough fortitude to wait another five hundred years. She felt her strength waning even as she breathed the stale, foreign air of this place.

Please. There was a word in Holly's song now. A demand. A plea.

Idiot girl. It might have taken Dedra three hundred years to master what the girl did in an instant, but that didn't mean she bowed to the ill-wrought message in the song. With sharp, honed precision, she shaped her own message and threw her notes into the bleak, waterless battleground.

This is insanity. You seek to save those of your blood. This is not the way.

It took only a heartbeat for Holly's song to change and reply. *It's the only way. You are the last, and I can't replace you. I am not so strong.* A pause. *And I don't know that there would ever be another.*

Dedra had lived with that fear for hundreds of years. Until the dreams had begun to visit a girl named after a foolish red berry. *Join me. We will be two.* She would stay as long as she could, honoring her new sister. Sharing the weight.

Holly's song just kept pushing. Singing of truth. Of shattering. Of reshaping and changing and setting those of their blood free. *Help me. For all those who will come of our line.* A dramatic pause, a single note hanging in the dark air. *And of his.*

Mikel.

His name broke something in Dedra, something she had thought long dead—and the tattered remnants of Mirena the kitchen girl came flowing through the cracks. Flooding, enormous love, rising in response to Holly's wild, reckless invitation. A willingness to take the gamble, to commit everything either of them had to breaking the back of the ancient plague that stalked their line.

Dedra's heart nearly stopped. She would die in this place, devoid of water, empty of life.

Mirena's life force rose higher.

———

HOLLY COULD HEAR all of them now. The entire theater vibrated with the old siren's monstrous resistance, with the energy of a thousand years of belief striking out in raging denial. With Holly's quietly, insistently sung response that this might be the very first moment in human history when the ending could be shifted. And with notes, felt but not heard, from a young girl who remembered what it was to hope.

This was the moment where the story would shift—or where it would fail.

A moment made possible by a kitchen girl's choice, a siren's tenacity, and a scholar princess who dared to demand a new ending.

With questing, reaching song, Holly invited them to join her in what she needed to do.

The old siren bowed her head, tears streaming down her face.

When she finally looked up, her eyes swam with grief and memory and wretched determination. And with the power of one who had once sung a song of life and death—and won.

Dedra tossed her hair behind her shoulders and began to sing. It wasn't something that played nicely with the notes Holly sang. Holly persisted, held her ground. Dedra had every right to take a good, long look at how she wanted to play this. This was a song of freedom. Of choice, even if lives depended on it.

A few more lines of breathtaking, raging torment—and then the siren's song hitched, and new notes came, ones that seemed to lift from the siren's throat softer than breath.

Holly's tears brimmed over. She knew she listened to the heartbreaking, heart-remaking music of a young girl who had sustained hope for a thousand years.

They were both there now, the siren and Mikel's beloved, and each had found the piece of the story that was theirs to tell. Holly closed her eyes, sinking into the trio of songs weaving their way into each other, filling her container, blazing trails of truth and hope and fear and love and need and belief into every molecule.

The glorious sounds of her sisters, showing up with all of who they were. Singing a curse to death, a man to life—and three women to freedom.

CHAPTER TWENTY-NINE

*H*olly slowed as she approached the sliding glass doors that would carry her into the hospital. Part of her didn't want to go through. It would pop the bubble of belief she'd been in since the last lines of her song had echoed out into the Inkspot theater and hovered there, all alone.

Mirena and Dedra gone, released into peace.

An ancient curse, dispersed into story.

And if she had threaded the needle right, a man on his way to health.

Inside the bubble she believed all that with all her heart. Facing the stark white walls of hospital corridors unending, it wasn't so easy to hold tight to conviction. Holly took shallow breaths as she walked, one hand wrapped around a tearstained pendant, trying not to inhale too deeply of the burgeoning fear that she had just gambled with a man's life.

And then she turned the corner into intensive care and nearly got trampled by a running, laughing, crying, babbling Monster.

"He wants pizza." Monster was jigging so hard, he almost knocked her over again. "He just woke up. His dad is in there and his sister and the doctors have to do some stuff and he wants pizza."

Holly could feel the hysterical giggles gathering, a storm of relief and joy and things far too complicated to name.

Instead, she reached for the keys in Monster's hand and gave him the kind of grin that only happened when life took a turn into a moment of glistening perfection and you were awake to see it. "I'll drive."

He beamed back at her and slung his arm through hers, a guy whose world had suddenly righted in the best of all possible ways.

She walked down the corridor with him, arm in arm, and hummed under her breath.

It had worked. They were free.

And this happy ending was apparently going to come loaded with tomato sauce and gooey cheese.

EPILOGUE

*H*olly unclipped her rope harness and slid off her climbing shoes, grateful to have her feet back on solid ground. "I can't believe Mirena climbed down that in a dress and her bare feet."

Jamie smiled and added his climbing harness to the pile. "Maybe we have the wrong cove."

They didn't. It had taken a year of research and intuition and way too much time zooming in on Google Earth, but this was the place. Holly took a deep breath and turned to face the water. The natural rock arch that created the entrance to the cove was unmistakable, but even without that, she would have known. She pointed at the rocks in the shallows on their left. "That was Dedra's favorite place to sit when the sun was shining." Or when she sang piercing laments for days at a time, but they hadn't come here to remember the sorrows.

Today was a day of celebration. One year ago exactly, she'd sung an ending—and in the days and months after, found her way to a beginning.

She felt Jamie's fingers slide into hers. Locating this place had been a big part of their first months together. "Still not too weirded out by this?"

He chuckled quietly. "I'm standing on a sunny private beach with a gorgeous woman and a backpack full of seriously yummy food. Not weirded out at all."

She had no idea why she was worried about that now. She'd had plenty of time to see his easy-going, pragmatic nature in action—it was a perfect foil for her storytelling, occasionally overdramatic self. "I guess if this was going to make you run, you'd have done it back when I first told you the story, huh?"

He grinned and tugged her toward the water. "Nah. I was way too focused on how your cheeks dimpled when you got embarrassed, and how you could sit at a table with tears running down your face and not even care."

He appreciated the strangest things. It had been their first date, and she'd told him the entire story over really spicy Thai noodles and copious amounts of chocolate mousse. His warm interest and level-headed calm hadn't shaken—not when they'd discovered that five-chili noodles really were suicidal, not when she'd told him the story of a medieval farmer and how his life was saved, and not when she'd sheepishly ordered a third helping of chocolate mousse.

She leaned into his warmth. "Those noodles made you cry too. Admit it."

"Nope. My sense of manhood requires that I don't weep over chilies. Just goopy stories." He grinned. "And my woman dressed up in a hot pink corset."

She groaned. "Don't remind me." This year's play had been carefully chosen—she'd leaned over Matteo's shoulder and made sure it was something with a meaty emotional role for the female lead. Unfortunately, she hadn't had any say in the costuming, and someone had borrowed pirate regalia from the theater two counties over, complete with the latest in sexy-pirate-mistress gear.

Apparently, she was doomed to a life of corsets.

There were worse fates.

She cuddled into Jamie's side. He'd cried over the story of Dedra and Mirena and the farmer who might have bestowed him his middle name, and that had tugged her into love a lot faster than she'd ever planned on going. "You listened so intently that night."

"Duh." He wrapped a warm, strong arm around her waist. "You'd finally worked up the guts to ask me out and I wasn't about to blow it."

For all that, they'd gone slowly. It had taken more than a few months to get over the whole predestined-lover thing. She'd wanted to be really sure she was making her own choices and not just reacting to the residual tremors of a dead curse or a matchmaking thousand-year-old siren. "You didn't blow it."

He bent over and kissed her, long and slow and lazy and tasting of sunshine. "I figured."

She looked out at the aquamarine waters of the cove, bathed in a lazy summer day. "I wonder if Dedra knows we're here."

His fingers brushed down her hair. "I thought you believed that she's gone."

She did. Mostly. There had been one dream, but Dedra had laughed and said Holly's subconscious had merely borrowed her to make a point.

Which hadn't depleted the power of the old siren's parting message at all. She had gazed down on the dream-shape of Jamie, asleep under a tree, his head nestled in Holly's lap, and then looked up, her eyes glistening with unshed tears. "You have the chance to love a good man."

The rest hadn't been said, but Holly had heard it anyhow.

She had the chance to love a good man—and not have to die for him.

Holly looked around the mellow, magical cove and sighed happily. She'd been smart enough to listen to her subconscious, or her thousand-year-old relative, whoever the true messenger had been, and it had turned out pretty well so far.

Which was part of what they were celebrating. They'd been here a week now, wandering around some of the local farms, putting their hands in the dirt, exploring ruins that might be old medieval villages or nothing at all.

And when she'd felt ready, her man had hefted his climbing gear and they'd come to find the cove.

"You're quiet." Jamie leaned down to kiss her again, the kind of gentle fondling that said he had some intentions for later, but they could take as long as they wanted getting there.

She grinned under his lips. "My mouth is kind of busy."

"That can be changed." He tucked her head under his chin and looked out at the water, chuckling as he felt her pouty face against his chest. "Is this where you tell me that our daughter's name is going to be Mirena?"

She felt a long, liquid pull as she tipped her head back to look at him. "We're naming our babies now, are we?" It felt strangely good, even if she had some things she wanted to be first.

Farmer. Playwright. Bard on the beach.

He shrugged, eyes easy and happy. "If you want to."

She read stories, analyzed them, put on a princess dress and acted them out. He lived them, one small moment at a time. "Not Mirena." That was in the past, and she wasn't hanging any name that soaked in meaning on a squalling infant. Kids should have a chance to become who they needed to be without getting dumped into a thousand-year-old story before they could walk. She smiled into his chest, pretty sure a kitchen girl would understand. "I might consider Monster, though."

Jamie laughed. "Because we need two of those in our lives?"

She grinned, thinking fondly of the guy who was their biggest fan—and, in the unlikely romance of the century, Jade's current main squeeze. Sausage guy and the catapult-building heiress to a corporate empire. Sometimes stories got totally out-written by real life. "I'm pretty sure they make our romance look really sane and normal."

"He's goopy in love." Jamie reached down and scooped her up, and then headed for the warm, beckoning waters. "And he's not the only one."

Holly tilted her head back into the sun, entirely happy. As she felt the cool waves rise up to meet them, she imagined she heard soft laughter off in the distance.

She assumed it came with a pair of smiling, blue-gray eyes.

THIS BOOK IS A STANDALONE, so there won't be sequels, but I have another singer for you! Turn the page for an excerpt from *Destiny's Song*. I think you'll enjoy Kish. :)

DESTINY'S SONG - CHAPTER ONE

"Yo, Kish."

I tried to resist the urge to strangle the guy calling my name. I was two seconds away from the door to my pod, a good mug of Tee's homebrew, and a bath in my entire water ration for the month. I turned to face the spike-haired teenager who had put his life between me and domestic bliss. "You want to die, Zee?"

Zane Lightbody, baby brother of my roommate and general all-around pest, blinked hard. "Singers aren't supposed to kill people."

KarmaCorp has all kinds of rules for its personnel. I'm not well known for following them. "I could make an exception."

"You won't." He looked almost sure. "Tee would be mad."

Tyra got mad about as often as the head of the Interplanetary Federated Commonwealth Council farted on vidscreen. "Is there a reason you're here, or can I strangle you now and leave you for compost?"

"Human bones go straight to the Growers, you know that. They need the calcium for mineralizing their soil mixes."

Only a dumb sixteen-year-old space brat lectures a would-be killer on the proper disposal of his body parts. I reached for the thumb-swipe on my pod door. "Go away, Zane. I'll see you Sunday at dinner." He and Tyra came from the most normal family in the galaxy. His dad made fried fish and rice every Sunday, and the whole family gathered at skydusk to eat and chat and catch up on each other's lives.

And ever since the first week of trainee school when I'd been summarily dumped into a co-pod with one Tyra Light-body, my presence was expected at Sunday dinner.

His eyes lit. "Cool—Mom will be really jazzed you're back." He clicked his heels together, activating the old-school air-wheels that had somehow not yet been outlawed in the walkways. "Catch you later. Tell Tee I said hi."

She could probably hear that for herself—her baby brother was seriously loud. I swiped a grimy thumb across the security pad, grateful when the door opened without complaining. It had been randomly denying us entry for months, and neither of us had the spare change to cough up for a tech. Besides, beating on the door usually worked. Eventually.

"Hey, Kish. Welcome home." The cheerful voice greeted me from the depths of our small pod. "Close the door gently, I've got bread rising."

I felt the grime and weariness of the trip start to lift off my shoulders. It had taken Tee a good six months after we'd moved in together to convince me to try her home-baked bread—it was made with microbes, for freak's sake. But something about the smell of those microbes cooking in the little box her dad had wired together as a home-leaving gift had eventually convinced me to live dangerously. I've been eating weird shit with microbes in it ever since.

I reached into my travel bag, inhaling the happy smells of yeast and friendship. "Get that stuff cooking—I brought you a present."

Her neatly coiffed head peeked around the corner that divided our tiny kitchen from the rest of the podspace. "Oooh, what?"

She had a little kid's love of treats and surprises. I held out the slightly squished tube, a lot worse for the wear after four days traveling inside one of my packed gravboots. "I brought you butter."

She squealed like a teenager at a vid concert. "The real stuff—are you serious? It must have cost two cycles' pay."

More than that, but I wasn't going to dampen her exuberance. "I figure there's enough there to take some to your dad, too." His fried fish was always good, but I'd had it a couple of times done up with real butter, and it had damn near put me into a coma.

"He'll be over the moon." She took the tube with reverent hands. "We're going to totally pig out first, though. Bread will be ready in an hour, so go get clean."

Tee's my best friend in the universe, but she can also be bossy as hell. "Yes, Mom."

"Whatever." She rolled her eyes and set down the butter, slinging herself into one of the ancient gel-chairs we called furnishings. "Stay grunge, see if I care. How'd the assignment go?"

The way they always went. Tricky with a helping of "oh, shit" on top. "When I got there, half the biome was ready to burn someone else at the stake." And that had been the saner half of the population. "It got worse while I was en route, apparently." When I'd left, it had just been your garden-variety revolt under way.

"Ouch." She shook her head, commiserating. "They never call you guys in fast enough."

All Fixers get sent into tough situations, but Singers have a special affinity for bringing people into harmony—it's one of the things our Talent does best. And Singers with wide vocal ranges get sent into situations where the parties are particularly far apart. I sighed. "In this case, I'm not sure there was anyone law-abiding enough left to make the call." A passing ship had radioed in the initial alert.

"A hard one, huh?" Tee's voice was full of sympathy.

"It went fine—it was just exhausting." When the people involved started kilometers apart on their desires, it was damned hard work to find the harmonics that would draw them together, and even more work to sustain those notes while stubborn heads and chakras contemplated the inevitable.

Tee has the personality for that kind of work—she's a born mediator. Me, I just try to outlast the idiots. I don't have much choice. Talents don't give a shit about personalities or anything else—they manifest wherever they damn well please. "I had to hold the final notes for almost two days."

She murmured all the right wordless things.

I leaned back, soaking in the satisfaction of telling a tale of woe to someone who really knew how to commiserate. "And then the jerk-off guy flying the tin can that brought me home missed his bounce by about ten nanos and put us through some really ugly negative-G acrobatics." Which had been hell on my aching lungs. The exhausted muscles between my ribs had been ready to decapitate the pilot where he sat. "I probably shouldn't have yelled at him." He'd totally deserved it, but my larynx didn't.

Tee winced. "Aww, your poor throat." She reached for a tiny bottle of aqua-blue liquid sitting on a nearby shelf. "Here, swallow a few drops of that when you go to bed tonight."

I'd do it in a heartbeat—her brews were magic. "Done, thanks. Got anything for my ribs?"

She smiled. "A good night's sleep."

That sounded seriously decent too. I closed my eyes, enjoying a moment of companionable silence. Tee knows when to talk and when to shut up, and I've always loved her for it. On a mining rock, the noise never stops. Silence was one of the first gifts KarmaCorp delivered to me. After that, the gifts had landed with more strings attached.

"Don't get too comfortable," said my roommate quietly.

I didn't like the sound of that. I squinted one eye open. "What's up?"

She shrugged. "Bean's been trying to reach you."

Yikes. The boss lady's assistant. They hadn't even let me get through Review yet, the mandatory tune-up every Fixer was subjected to when she came off a job—Yesenia insisted on it. They'd check to see that my vocals hadn't developed any strange wobbles while I'd been yelling at the shithead space pilot.

I could have told them not to bother, but nobody disobeyed the edicts of Yesenia Mayes, whether they agreed with her or not. The woman ran the KarmaCorp presence in this corner of the Commonwealth with a strict and arrogant fist—but based on the stories I'd heard from Fixers in other parts of the galaxy, she also ran a tight ship free of most of the crap that has infected bureaucracies since time began. And while I'd never seen her show mercy, I'd never seen her be overtly cruel, either—and a mining-asteroid brat like me has a pretty good nose for such things.

However, none of that made her any less scary.

"Yo, Earth to Kish."

I snorted. Neither of us has ever been anywhere near the planet that gave birth to our ancestors out of some sort of primordial ooze. "I'm still here. And since it's about to be after hours, I vote you raid your brew stash."

She grinned. "What brew stash?"

I rolled my eyes. "What, you got all legal and proper while I was gone?" Not likely. Tee is sweet and gentle and a goddess because she puts up with me, but she's not as much of a pushover as she looks. She flexes the rules with the best of us, and then bats her flirty brown eyes at the people in charge and generally manages to stay out of trouble. It's hard to hate her for it, though—she's too damn nice. Always has been, even in the early days of trainee school when I'd been ready to chew nails and hated everyone who breathed within a hundred meters of me.

My first friend.

I took the clear glass of light purple brew she handed my way and sighed in deep contentment. It was good to be home.

CHAPTER TWO

"*H*ey, Kish—welcome back." The cheerful face of Yesenia's assistant peered out from my tablet. "You got time to go through a few things?"

I had a belly full of Tee's homemade bread and the yogurt she made from coconut milk and hoarded like gold bars. Even the boss couldn't rock me out of my happy lassitude. "Sure thing." I swung my feet up on a gel-stool and settled in. Chats with Bean were never brief. I grinned at one of the people I liked best in the galaxy. "Any of the new trainees call you Lucy yet?"

Yesenia's executive assistant and right hand had been born Lucinda Coffey. Her grandmothers and the occasional dumb trainee called her Lucy—the rest of the Commonwealth called her Bean.

She winced. "Not yet."

Whoever did would get a friendly warning. After that, they'd get a visit. Fixers took care of their own, and Bean was as universally loved as the drink she'd named herself after.

Which was a fair feat when you were often the messenger for a woman who ate small children for breakfast and reduced grown men to quivering puddles frequently enough that every bartender on Stardust Prime recognized the symptoms.

I eyed my tablet, vaguely embarrassed to be woolgathering. "You got my report, yeah?" I'd filed it two minutes before docking, and written it in the ten minutes before that.

"Got it." Bean nodded solemnly. "It's a little sparse."

More than a little. "I'm economical with my words."

"I'll pass that along to Yesenia if she has concerns."

I snorted, knowing that was an entirely idle threat, at least in my case. "I brought you back some flowers." Bean had an unreasonable fondness for things that died in less than a week, and the rebellious biome had been lousy with a bunch of varieties I'd never seen.

Her entire face softened. "Zane delivered them a few minutes ago, thank you."

Hopefully Tee's baby brother hadn't smushed them against more than a few walls on his way. "Did they arrive in one piece?"

She chuckled. "Mostly."

Damn, I needed a better delivery service.

"So hey, can I get you to drop in on a trainee class while you're here?" Her voice was almost pleading. "You don't have to give a talk or anything, just do a question-and-answer session. Let them see a real, live Singer in the flesh."

Poor Bean had the thankless job of trying to keep trainee school from entirely sucking. "Haven't I already done that twice this rotation?"

"Different class. This is the third-years—they're harder to impress."

And past the trauma of being yanked away from home, which was hard, even for the ones who were willing. I hadn't been one of the willing ones, which was why Bean often sent me to visit the youngest classes. "What am I supposed to do to entertain them, Andalusian tap dance?"

She grinned. "Just be yourself. You can wow them with your command presence and steady temperament."

I laughed. We both knew I'd missed the lines where those were handed out.

Her head tilted a little to the left. "Remember what a big deal it was when one of the Fixers came to your class fresh off an assignment?"

That was playing dirty. I'd been eleven the first time it had happened, still coated in several layers of mining-brat grime and looking for a way back home. The woman who'd come to visit with us had been a Dancer, and by the time she'd left, something far less putrid and homesick had been running through my veins. "I'm not going to Sing for them."

Bean snorted. "That's what you always say."

It's what I always meant. I had no willpower against shiny eyes and wistful faces, grimy or not. "Just let me know when to be there."

"I will." She held a couple of fingers up to her screen cam. "Thanks."

I had no willpower against kind hearts, either. "Is that all you need?" It was exactly an hour after breakfast, but I felt a nap coming on. Travel lag is such a strange beast.

"Nope." Bean sounded apologetic. "I have the briefing file for your new assignment. Sending it now."

I tapped on the small, blinking folder on my screen, shaking my head at the name emblazoned across the top.

Lakisha Drinkwater—after twenty-five years, you'd think it would feel like mine. It was a nod to two of the many heritages flowing in the mongrel blood of my adoptive family, and an overlong mouthful of a name nobody ever bothered to use. Those who know me well call me Kish. Everyone else calls me Singer, because that's my function in the universe. What they call me behind my back is their problem. Singers don't tend to make a lot of friends—people get a bit twitchy when you can open your mouth, sing a note or two, and screw with their lives.

Or so says the mythology Yesenia works hard to feed, anyhow. She wants the Fixers respected—and in the language she understands, that means she wants us feared.

I spread the folder's contents out on my screen, scanning for the data that mattered. As usual, KarmaCorp buried the important stuff in a sea of background material I could have easily looked up for myself on the GooglePlex. My eyes hit the first critical piece of information and paused. "Where the hell's Bromelain III?" I knew most of the Federation planets in this quadrant. "Don't tell me I have to ride in a sleep bucket." I'd only done cryo-travel once and I'd hated every oblivious second of it.

"Nope. It's only six days away. One of the outpost colonies."

That could mean anything from lawless to fourth generation and ready to join the Federated Commonwealth as a grown-up. It also explained why I'd never heard of them. Fixers rarely got sent to the colony planets—not enough happened there that could shake the galaxy's core. They were more the province of the Anthros. The rest of us got held firmly behind the borders that kept the inner planets sheltered and safe, and the colonies free to innovate and find their own way until they got stable enough to join the club.

I scanned a few more lines and files—and then two words in red registered. "Get out." I squinted at Bean's tiny face in the top corner of my tablet. "Why the heck is this 'Ears Only'?"

"You know I can't answer that."

I knew she wasn't supposed to, but Bean usually managed to work around the rules when it mattered.

I enlarged the video app to full-screen. "What's going on?"

"Can't tell you." She looked apologetic and a little squirmy. "I don't actually know all the details. Yesenia can see you any time this afternoon."

A squirmy Bean was disturbing—Yesenia willing to fit me into her schedule was terrifying. "When's a good slot?"

Her eyes scanned something that I assumed was the boss lady's calendar. "How about right after lunch?" She glanced sideways and spoke under her breath. "She's been on a bit of a tear lately."

I snorted. "When isn't she?"

Bean choked on a laugh. "Gotta run, I hear the next meeting arriving. Thanks again for the flowers."

Some people were really easy to please. "No big. See you this aft." I signed off and flipped my tablet over to GooglePlex mode. Time to do some digging on Bromelain III, and not in the nice, manicured fields of the KarmaCorp briefing materials.

CHAPTER THREE

J yawned as I crossed the threshold into the offices of the woman who ran KarmaCorp in this part of the galaxy. Should have stopped for some caffeine. Dealing with Yesenia was tricky enough without the loggy brain that always hit me after long-haul space flights and late-morning naps. "Afternoon, Bean."

The small, lithe woman behind the desk rolled back the balance ball she used as a chair and bounced up. Her dreads bobbed madly as she closed the distance and placed a big, hard kiss on my cheek. "Kish! You look like hell. Didn't Tyra feed you and make you take a nap?"

I grinned, well used to the unnecessary mothering. "She did. I saved a piece of bread for you." I dug in my bag to rescue it before it turned to crumbs.

Bean opened a corner of the small container and inhaled deeply—and then her eyes shot open. "You got real butter?"

"Ssh." I laughed, quietly. "You want to share that with half the habitat?"

She tore off the lid and popped a good chunk of it into her mouth. "Nope." She chewed twice and closed her eyes, humming a note of quiet bliss.

That was better for my loggy brain than caffeine. "Boss lady ready for me?"

Bean waved her hand vaguely in the direction of Yesenia's inner sanctum.

I took that as invitation and stepped toward the door. It slid open moments before I got there. Yesenia came around her gleaming desk, hand out in royal greeting. "Welcome back, Journeywoman Drinkwater."

The urge to tweak her was irresistible. "Gods, Yesenia—when are you going to call me Kish like the rest of the solar system?"

Her eyes glinted sharp steel. "I very rarely seek to be like the rest of the solar system."

Truer words were never said—and I wasn't dumb enough to mess with the steel in her eyes twice. "I hear you have a new assignment for me."

"Always straight to business." She sighed, which froze me in my boots. "I used to be like you, mind always focused from one assignment to the next."

Yesenia was a Fixer legend, one of the few Travelers who'd done her stint and could still talk in complete sentences. I didn't know whether she started out tough as nails, but she'd certainly finished that way. Regret wasn't in her vocabulary. I stepped very carefully, on high alert for exploding space debris. "KarmaCorp trains us to focus."

"Yes, we do." Something in her demeanor shifted. "And you do it very well, Lakisha—I never meant to suggest otherwise. What do you know of your next assignment?"

I knew that a backwoods planet needed a Fixer—and I knew the situation had somehow merited enough attention to get labeled high security. "The file said 'Ears Only.'"

"It did." She waited a long moment, her face the impassive mask that could start a miscreant babbling in two seconds flat. "Lucinda didn't fill you in any further?"

I didn't throw friends under mining carts, and this time, Bean had known very little. "She told me Bromelain III was an outpost colony."

Yesenia raised an unimpressed eyebrow. "A little weak on your quadrant geography, are you?"

There was no point trying to explain standard human weakness to a woman who had none. "I've learned a little more since I got the file."

She tapped her fingers on a tablet that could probably turn mine into a pile of metal shards without even trying hard. "Other than a quick review while you were in contact with Lucinda this morning, I have no record of you accessing the briefing materials."

Knowing KarmaCorp tracked my every move was far less annoying than having it shoved in my face. "You might look at the records of my GooglePlex activity since then—I'm sure those will be more informative."

My prickly tone had Yesenia's eyebrow sliding up again, more dangerously this time. She took a seat in a narrow, angular chair in front of her desk and gestured to its twin. "Sit."

I didn't want to, but that was a piss-poor battle to pick. I was a grown-up now, not a fourth-year trainee who'd been caught greasing hatch locks. I made myself as comfortable as possible in a chair that clearly didn't want people sitting on it for long. "These are new."

"They are indeed." Her face gave nothing away.

I was too damn travel lagged and grouchy to keep my best manners in place. "If you put a bunch of these in the detention pod, trainees would probably be a lot better behaved."

"I'll take it under advisement."

It was way past time to stop talking about the furniture. "Intel on Bromelain III is sparse. Good climate, large grasslands sustaining the oxygen levels." Which mattered because people locked up in astrosuits all day long got really jumpy. BroThree, as the locals called it, was probably a pretty mellow place compared to my last assignment. "Eligible for Federated planet status soon." Which was a big deal, and the only clue I'd found about why I might be headed that way. Federation status was the doorway into the inner circle of power, governance, and everything else that mattered in the galaxy—at least according to the people already in there.

My boss was doing an excellent imitation of a statue. An impatient and possibly displeased one.

I tried to think what else I'd dug up that might matter. "Not much chatter on the sim waves. Inheritor planet, so governance is pretty straightforward."

"Ah." Yesenia leaned forward, interrupting my spiel. Statue awakened. "Tell me what you learned about the Lovatts."

Other than knowing they were the family that ran the place, not much. I wondered what I'd missed. "Standard Inheritor structure—ruling title passes to the most-suited child, as voted on by the council and citizens."

She nodded her head once and looked marginally less

displeased. "Did you know that in Earth-based feudal societies, it was the firstborn male child who inherited?"

I was no Anthro, but that sounded dumb as rocks. "Doesn't that just provide incentive for the firstborn to end up dead?"

"Indeed."

My brain was sending high-alert signals again. There was something going on here besides a history lesson. "Is the Inheritor Elect in danger?" That was an unusual assignment for a Singer, but I'd had stranger.

"Not at all." Yesenia's fingers tapped a riff on her knee. "Devan Lovatt was chosen most suited for leadership at the council plenarium last year. The vote was unanimous."

I shifted gingerly in the chair. "So he's the heir apparent."

"It wasn't a difficult vote—his sisters have made clear that they aren't interested."

As I'd learned at ten years old, lack of interest doesn't always get you off the hook. "Do they show any aptitude?"

Yesenia inclined her head, teacher to adequately bright student. "One shows significant talent with solar mechanics, and the other is pregnant with her fourth child and writes a well-respected series of vidbooks for children."

"A family with varied skills." And ones that didn't provide a lot of clues about why KarmaCorp was interested in the political machinations of a backwater colony. "I assume the sister with engineering skills is on a ship somewhere." Good solar mechanics were literally worth their bodyweight in gold.

"She is, for the past two years now. Her mentors report admirable progress."

And somewhere in there might lie the reason that a Fixer was being sent to an outpost colony. Any genes that could produce solar mechanics would have earned themselves a place on KarmaCorp's radar. I didn't ask for details—there was no chance in any planet's hells that I'd get an answer, and I didn't really want one. Commonwealth politics were as convoluted and labyrinthine as it got. I was just a Singer who did what I was told, and very glad to keep it that way.

Time to get the down low on my assignment and get out of here. "Forgive my lack of patience, Director, but why are you sending me to Bromelain III?"

"You'll be observing Devan Lovatt."

I raised an eyebrow of my own, thoroughly confused. Fixers didn't generally get sent to babysit, even for royalty.

Yesenia's hands played that riff on her knee again. "And a young woman by the name of Janelle Brooker."

Sometimes notes sound bad even before they're played. "And who would she be, exactly?"

"She's the middle daughter of another well-respected colony family." The boss lady's game face did nothing to calm my gut. "The Brookers can trace their roots all the way back to the grain fields of Saskatchewan."

That bit of geography I did know. Canada hadn't been the first of Earth's countries into space, but they'd been one of the last left with water and land that could grow things, and that had fueled their colonization of half the star system. A country of pioneers used to cold and isolation, they'd had the right DNA for space exploration. That made the Brookers at least minor relations to galactic royalty, and Yesenia wanted to make sure I knew it.

This was getting stinkier than a compost droid. We had two young people on some backwoods space rock, and either their family connections or some situation they'd managed to get tangled up in had qualified them for a high-security KarmaCorp intervention. "Did they get themselves into something sticky?"

"In a manner of speaking."

I sat quietly, not at all sure I wanted to hear what came next.

"Our astrologers believe the two are compatible and intended to marry."

I tried not to gape, shocked to the core that they'd pointed a StarReader at two kids on some outpost planet. Astrologers were a credit a dozen all over the galaxy, but KarmaCorp employed the ones who ended up right most of the time—and there weren't nearly enough of them. They were the company's most valuable commodity. "What, I'm supposed to keep the two of them out of trouble before the wedding?"

"No. Apparently the two parties are not yet convinced of their future together."

That was crazy. "Nobody argues with a KarmaCorp StarReader."

Yesenia's lips pursed. "They aren't to be told. No one is. That information will not leave this office."

That was even crazier.

She eyed me with a look that regularly froze the blood of people two decades my senior. "That directive comes from the highest levels, and you will comply with it, Journeywoman."

That could only mean StarReader edict. One that likely had far more tentacles than a simple marriage on some boon-docks colony. I grimaced—and then the other shoe landed, the whole reason a Singer was being pulled into this mess. To create harmony where none existed. "No. No way."

Yesenia's eyebrows warned of impending death should I choose to keep up my foolish babble.

The knots in my gut cowered and kept talking anyhow. "That's insane." And far, far worse than babysitting.

"That is for others to decide." She was Yesenia Mayes in full throttle now, and no one would dare to cross her. "You will do your job, Singer, and you will do it with all the skill, talent, and training at your disposal."

Of course I would—there was never any other choice. Fixers did what we were told.

But sweet holy shit. I was being sent off to a backwater rock—to be a matchmaker.

READ the rest of *Destiny's Song*.

Made in the USA
Columbia, SC
24 October 2020

23414502R00131